DARK NIGHT
OF THE SOUL

A NOVEL

GARY REILLY

Running Meter Press

DENVER

Published by
Running Meter Press
2509 Xanthia St.
Denver, CO 80238
Publisher@RunningMeterPress.com
720 328 5488

Cover art by John Sherffius
Composition by D.K. Luraas

ISBN: 978-0-9847860-9-1

Library of Congress Control Number: 2014950722

First Edition 2014

Printed in the United States of America

INTRODUCTION

We launched the first novel in Gary Reilly's unique series about Denver taxi driver Brendan Murphy, a.k.a. "Murph," in the summer of 2012. We had no idea where this was going—or for how long. Nearly thirty months after *The Asphalt Warrior* hit the streets, we have reached the sixth novel in the series, *Dark Night of the Soul*. To date, two of Gary's books have been named finalists for the Colorado Book Awards and all have landed on the local best-seller list.

We'd like to briefly delay your enjoyment of Murph's next trek around the colorful streets of Denver and take a moment to offer a heartfelt thanks to many who have helped us along the way.

Due in part to Gary's growing fan base and also to the fact that Gary had many brothers and sisters, Running Meter Press has received generous gifts to continue the ongoing effort. There is lots of work left. Five more "Murph" novels remain unpublished. Earlier this year, we published the first of Gary Reilly's accounts of his service during the Vietnam era. *The Enlisted Men's Club* introduced us to another memorable Reilly character, Private Palmer, and two more stories remain in that saga. In addition, there are another dozen (or so) titles in a wide variety of genres that Gary Reilly left behind in his steamer trunk. We will be busy for years to come.

Today, there is an ever-expanding team behind Running Meter Press and we need to thank them: Peg Ondrak, Lynn Setzer, Gregg and Jeannie Haycraft, Greg Pulliam, Paula Sandoval, Joanne Krieg, Craig Reilly, Joseph Nigg, Esther Muzzillo, Daniel Reilly, Marilyn Reilly, Judy Waite, Theresa Peterson, Craig Carver, Bob Tucker, Bob Krieger, Tom Geimer, Mike McLanahan, Greg Hill, Dennis Gallagher, Denis Berckefeldt, and Julie Ondrak. And of course in particular we must thank Sherry Peterson, who supported Gary's writing dream in so many ways for decades. There is also a whole team of people who help with these publications—and whose support is invaluable. These include editor Mira Perrizo, designer Nick Zelinger, artist John Sherffius, e-book specialist Gail Nelson, the fine book publicity team at JKS Communications, and web designer Anita Austin. We must also thank the Tattered Cover staff and our friends at Broadway Book Mall—Ron and Nina Else and Dean Wyant, too—for all their generous and ongoing support.

Gary Reilly's fans continue to grow. We couldn't be more thrilled.

As any good asphalt warrior might say, "Onward!"

Mike Keefe and Mark Stevens
Running Meter Press

CHAPTER 1

My alarm clock went off at six a.m. that Monday morning. I immediately hit the snooze button. I had been up the previous evening thinking about trying to write a novel, and nothing drains a writer more than thinking about trying to write. A lot of it has to do with the energy it takes to not watch television. Not watching television is like going to a bar and not drinking. That's as far as I can take the analogy, because I've never done that.

But as I sat in my apartment the previous evening staring at the blank screen of my TV, I subconsciously got the urge to turn it on. I could feel every muscle in my body aching to get up and walk across the living room and pick up the remote control, which I had purposely set on top of the TV to keep it out of my reach. I managed to resist the urge to get up, but it took an enormous amount of effort. It reminded me of the Charles Atlas course advertised on the backs of comics when I was a kid.

I'll admit it. At the age of ten my dream was to kick sand in the face of a bully. I had tried that once at the age of eight, however at that time I did not possess a thorough grounding in the art of modern advertising.

Later on, while reading a comic in the hospital, I realized what I had done wrong: I had not sent Charles Atlas ten cents. The ten cents was to cover the return postage on an introductory booklet for his muscle-building course—or so he claimed. After I was released from Wichita General I asked my Maw if she would give me the necessary ten cents. She said she would be glad to give me ten cents if I mowed the lawn.

I mulled this over for a few days, then came to the conclusion that it just might be worth it. If things worked out the way I planned, I might be able to extract revenge against Danny Doyle. His was the face into which, in my marketing-and-distribution naiveté, I had sent a spray of sand. This was at a place called Courtney Davis, a swimming resort that apparently no longer exists in Wichita. It was like a Club Med for Jay-hawkers. Why did I kick sand into Danny Doyle's face? It's a long story but I think stupidity covers all the bases. Briefly, he had knocked an ice-cream cone out of my hand while roughhousing with his pals.

I was always amazed that bullies had pals. Where did they get pals? Did a kid have to apply for friendship with a bully? What were the requirements? Was there an annual fee?

Anyway, it took me two hours to mow the yard and by the time I was finished I no longer wanted muscles. That was the end of my business association with Charles Atlas. But when I turned thirteen, I learned the secret of "dynamic tension." This was one of those secrets that ran the grapevine of adolescent boys. Word on the street said that some kid had actually sent away for the Charles Atlas course, and had blown the lid off dynamic tension. I suspected it was Danny Doyle. The secret consisted of flexing your muscles real hard, which was about as disappointing as learning it was impossible to literally "throw your voice" with a gadget that cost a buck. I don't want to talk about that.

Nevertheless, I immediately set out to flex my muscles—in secret of course. I didn't want any trouble with the U.S. Patent Office. I didn't have that many muscles when I was thirteen but I did manage to flex the ones I found. I was primarily determined to develop gigantic biceps and pecs, so I spent hours in the bathroom behind the locked door flexing my muscles in front of the mirror. After two days of this grueling workout I did not detect any visible signs of progress, which led to my loss of faith in comics.

But since I had given my Maw the impression that I was willing to mow the lawn, I earned forty cents a month during the summer of my thirteenth year. I ate twelve chocolate sundaes in twelve weeks, not including my usual sundaes. By the time school rolled around I had a gained a pound of muscle in my wrists from pushing the lawnmower. Also five pounds of fat on what appeared to be my stomach. On the night I weighed my wrists on the bathroom scale, me ol' Dad walked past the doorway and saw me, but didn't say anything.

Anyway, I was sitting there in my living room staring at the TV and found myself fighting the instinctive reflexes of my muscles. My body wanted to get out of the chair, but I wouldn't let it. This went on for half an hour. It was just like going to the gym where I had once paid two hundred and fifty dollars to walk through the front door twice.

At the end of the half-hour I was covered with a sheen of sweat, and I was breathing heavily.

But I had spent so much time fighting my muscles that I forgot to think up the plot of a novel. It didn't matter though because I was so exhausted that I didn't have the energy to cross the living room and turn on my RamBlaster 4000 personal computer and wait for it to warm up. It's the waiting that kills you. Instead, I staggered into my bedroom, kicked off my Keds, and collapsed into bed.

When the alarm went off the next morning I hit the snooze button. It was set for ten minutes. Unfortunately, after the radio came back on I slept through the rock songs. I truly was exhausted from my Herculean writing labors of the night before.

Suddenly "Jailhouse Rock" erupted and my eyes popped open. Whenever I hear Elvis Presley I immediately begin making calculations, trying to discern whether it's the pre-army Elvis or the post-army Elvis. I like the pre. In fact I have a theory that the man who came home from Germany in 1962 was not the real Elvis Presley, but I don't want to get into that and neither do the gate guards at Area 51.

I stared at the ceiling for a while, then I casually rolled over and glanced at the clock, and nearly had a heart attack. It was seven twenty-five. Normally I sign out my cab at the Rocky Mountain Taxicab Company (RMTC) at seven a.m. I immediately panicked and got out of bed. I staggered into the living room and did something I had never done before in my life, which was to make a telephone call at dawn.

There is a rule at Rocky Cab that says a driver is allowed thirty minutes to pick up his assigned taxi or it will be given to someone else looking for a day lease—unless the assigned driver phones in to let them know he is coming. I had to call Rollo, the man in the cage who is in charge of handing out keys, and let him know I was coming. I had never gotten along very well with Rollo, but when he answered the phone he didn't give me any jive. He said he would hold cab #123 until I arrived.

It sort of annoyed me to have to talk to Rollo like a normal person because I like to employ subtle forms of sarcasm when speaking to him. I felt cheated.

After I hung up the phone I rushed around my apartment getting dressed. It infuriated me. Not that I'm opposed to getting dressed, but I hadn't rushed around in panic in a long time. I did do that a lot in the army where they had things like sergeants and bugles, but that was a quarter-century ago, which is a long time to not panic.

I grabbed my plastic briefcase and walked out the back door, locked up my crow's nest, and hurried down the fire escape. I hopped into my Chevy, fired it up and drove onto 13th Avenue.

I felt foolish as I negotiated the dawn streets of Denver. Everybody was heading for work, the rush hour was on, and I was a part of it. I felt like Jason Robards. It wasn't a good feeling.

I arrived at the motor at ten minutes to eight. The parking lot was dead. The seven a.m. shift-change was long over, i.e., the bustling of asphalt warriors climbing out of night-shift cabs and the day-shift drivers replacing them like soldiers at the parapets of the Alamo. Well. Something like that.

The silence was eerie as I headed for the door of the on-call room.

Normally I like silence but I can do without eeriness. It reminded me of being late for school, the most gut-wrenching thing that can happen to a first-grader. I was glad to get inside where the eeriness was normal, especially with Rollo seated behind the glass window of the cage eating a donut. Rollo bears a resemblance to half the character actors who ever made B movies, my two favorites being Sidney Greenstreet and Andy Divine. Take your pick—there's plenty more where they came from. Anybody here remember Eugene Pallette?

Rollo is the man in charge of Rocky drivers in the daytime. He's like a line producer on a movie set. The man in the cage wields a lot of power in a cab company, in the way that a bottleneck wields power over anything that gets stuck anywhere. Use your imagination.

I felt foolish walking up to the cage almost an hour late. Rollo was now like a school teacher. Even before I opened my mouth, he knew he had won. I could tell he knew because he didn't lord it over me. You may find this hard to believe, but cab driving is one of the few arenas of my life where I am actually competent. I can't offhand think of the others. But when I screw up in the cab arena, it's hang-my-head time. I waited for Rollo to toss a little malicious condescension my way. Standard operating procedure. I was like a guy in an old-fashioned duel who fires his pistol first and then has to stand there like a doofus while his opponent takes careful aim.

I set my plastic briefcase on the ledge and made a big bustling production out of pulling my seventy dollars from my T-shirt pocket and counting it out while Rollo just gazed at me. But I knew exactly what the bastard was doing. He was waiting for me to chuckle and say, "Guess I overslept," which I proceeded to say, otherwise he would have instigated the protocol of condescension and crushed my ego to a pulp. He's a stickler for the conventions of the duel. But he just smiled approvingly and took the seventy dollars and handed me my key and trip-sheet. Then he said, "Keillor is scheduled to sign out your cab at seven this evening, Murph."

I nodded. I would be pulling an eleven-hour shift while paying for a twelve-hour shift. This is one of those "cracks" that people often talk about things falling through.

There is simply nothing Rocky Cab can do for a driver who shows up late for work. He has to pay for the full shift. Rocky's sole source of income is lease payments, and if a man can't pay, there are plenty of other losers waiting to take his place. Fortunately, the turnover rate of losers at Rocky is so high that even if I got fired I could reapply and be back on the road in two hours.

"I'll be here at seven," I said, even though convention did not require that I say it. But this was Rollo's finest hour. He gets one of those every couple of months. I get my share, too. Rollo and I approach our mutual revulsion in the way that WWI pilots engaged in aerial combat over the fields of Flanders. We're a couple of goddamn gentlemen.

CHAPTER 2

I found #123 parked near the doors of the garage where the mechanics were busy fixing the cabs that the newbies had wrecked in one way or another. Sometimes body damage, sometimes broken transmissions. I guess I don't need to tell you the many things that can happen to an automobile. I'm going to stick my neck out here and assume that you own one. Or at least you've wrecked one.

I checked the body for dents and dings. No problem. Then I popped the hood for Monday morning first-echelon maintenance. I checked the oil and water and transmission fluid. The water was low, so I went into the garage and got a bucket of radiator mix and carried it out to the cab and poured a quart in. You have to stay on top of radiators. Newbies drive my cab a lot and they don't always pull proper maintenance. After fastening the radiator cap, I borrowed a tire gauge from a mechanic and checked the air.

A-OK.

I was an hour late for work but I wasn't rushing around now. I was "going with the flow." No use trying to make up for lost time. Time is one thing that's never on your side when you have a job. I had learned from experience that I could rush around and bust my ass to get out on the road, yet come April 15th I would still pay the same old cut to Uncle. You never win and you never lose in the taxi game.

That's what one part of my brain was telling me—the intelligent part, I guess you could say. The other part was screaming at me to get moving! I don't know what that part of my brain is called. Gym coach.

Nun. Sergeant. But I ignored it, just as I ignored their real-life counter-parts when I was little, or young, depending on the time frame. I knew there was no reason to worry because I could easily make up an hour's worth of money. That's part of the beauty of cab driving. You can make money if you actually work.

I was ambivalent about this of course. I didn't sign up to be a taxi driver in order to work, and I didn't care that much about money. In truth, I didn't really know why I was at the cab company. I had to stop and think about it. I did so after I closed the hood and climbed in and got ready to call the dispatcher to let him know I was on the asphalt. I finally decided I was there because I had to be. That's my all-purpose excuse for everything.

I picked up the microphone and waited a moment for the dispatcher to stop yelling at a newbie, then I pressed the button and said, "One twenty-three."

"One twenty-three," the dispatcher said.

"I'm headed out," I said. That wasn't proper radio protocol. There's a phrase you're supposed to use when signing on with the dispatcher but I couldn't remember what it was. And anyway, I was doing what all people do who have been doing things for a long time. I was pretending that the rules didn't apply to me. I was pretending I was "special."

"You're late, Murph," the dispatcher said.

He's a card. He likes to rib me. I've never seen his face. He's just a voice, a shadowy figure speaking to me from the radio room on the second floor of RMTC.

"Up yours," I said.

"If you want an el-two, I can arrange it," he replied.

I didn't respond. I hung up the mike. My relationship with the dispatcher is different from my relationship with Rollo. It's more dangerous. It's a miracle that the dispatcher lets me get away with that crap. An L-2 means you have to go back inside and get reamed out.

I headed for a 7-11 to gas up and buy a cup of coffee and a Twinkie. I didn't rush. I put myself into a state of mind that I call "cabbie consciousness." It's sort of like Transcendental Meditation but doesn't involve a mantra. In fact it's more like watching television. I just pretend that whatever I'm doing at the current moment in time is real, as opposed to what I ought to be doing, which is rushing to buy gas, picking up fares, making up for lost time, and generally acting mature and responsible.

Give me a break.

I arrived at 7-11 but had to wait five minutes for a line of cars at the gas pump. This shattered my calm. The 7-11 where I gas up is normally not very busy. It's located at what you might call "the edge of the city," which is in north Denver near the viaducts. Most people are afraid to get out of their cars in that part of town. There's something about viaducts that give people the willies. But elevated roadways don't bother me. I just keep my back to them and concentrate on squeezing out the unleaded. I do keep my eyes closed, but that's because the fumes make my whites red, and I have found that red-eyed cab drivers give fares the willies.

After I hung up the pump I strolled into the 7-11.

And froze.

There were fifteen customers standing in line. I looked outside. Maybe three cars were parked in the lot. Where the hell did all these time-destroyers come from? I rushed to the coffee machine and filled a paper cup, then snatched a Twinkie and raced to the end of the line before anybody else magically appeared out of nowhere. There's nothing that infuriates me more than a long line at 7-11. Losing my TV remote runs a close second, so you can imagine how I felt that morning.

I then did something I almost never do. I glanced at my wristwatch. I hate Time in general and clocks in particular, but I had learned that a cab driver has to own a watch. This relates to picking up fares on time. Need I say more? But I sure as hell never looked at a wristwatch while buying a Twinkie. The whole scene left a sour taste in my mouth. I almost put the Twinkie back.

I didn't recognize the clerk. He looked like a newbie. Young. Nervous. Trying to figure out the process of selling a money order to an old lady. The old lady was counting out pennies from a change purse.

I nearly collapsed mentally. My gas tank was full, so I couldn't put the unleaded back on the shelf and flee. I was trapped. Everybody else in line was holding Fritos and candy bars and bottled water. They could have said to hell with it and put their items back on the shelves and walked out. So why didn't they?

I did my best to encourage them. I began sighing with impatience. It didn't work. Each customer had staked out his private square of tile and was standing firm, waiting for the old lady to get the exact change right down to the last corroded Lincoln head. Old ladies do this in order to "help" clerks. Thank God taxi meters round off to twenty cents. It reduces my mental collapses by a factor of five.

I won't describe the time destruction engaged in by the customers ahead of me. I won't do to you what they did to me. Let's just say it was a quarter to nine before I got back into my cab, took a sip of cold coffee, and vowed that as long as I lived I would never again fill my gas tank without scouting the terrain for signs of enemy presence. Fortunately I knew how to do this. I saw a training film in the army.

I placed the dead joe in my cup holder, then started the engine and pulled away from the 7-11. It made me feel bad to have ill feelings toward my favorite store. I'm old enough to remember when 7-11 stores actually opened at 7 and closed at 11, and believe me, brother, that was a quantum leap in the evolution of Denver. It made me feel like I possessed an embarrassment of riches every time I strolled into a 7-11 at 10:55 to buy a pack of smokes. I was taken down a peg, though, when I visited my brother Gavin in California and discovered that liquor stores—not bars but liquor stores—stayed open past two a.m. That's when I realized

Albert Einstein was wrong. "Relativity" wasn't the right word. "Pathos" nailed it. But I came back to Denver anyway. Apartment prices here are peanuts relative to the West Coast.

As I drove away from the 7-11, I saw a man waving frantically to me. He was standing on a corner where a small park was located. No shops or stores or even houses nearby. He was a "pedestrian." Normally I never pick up pedestrians who try to flag me down. It's a safety thing. Cabbies sometimes get robbed by people who don't phone the RMTC dispatcher for a ride. If you pick someone up off the street, the company has no idea that you've got a fare in your backseat, which is the way robbers like it.

But I was almost two hours behind schedule and I hadn't made a dime, so I literally heaved a sigh of resignation and pulled over to the curb. I figured I was safe. He looked okay. Well-dressed. Mid-thirties. Nicely groomed. Ted Bundy looked that way when he escaped from the Aspen jail.

The pedestrian leaned into my window. "I'm only going a few blocks but I missed my bus and I'm late for work, can you take me there?"

"Climb in," I said. A three-dollar ride at best. It didn't matter. I was going in that direction anyway. Three bucks is three bucks said John Jacob Astor, probably.

A couple minutes later I pulled over to the curb. The guy handed me a twenty.

I looked at it.

Then I looked at the meter.

Three bucks.

Suddenly three bucks wasn't three bucks. It was Mount St. Helena. "Do you have anything smaller than this?" I said. I had only twenty dollars worth of change on me. I do carry at least two twenties in my billfold at all times—what I call my "amateur" stash—but that's for emergencies, and they wouldn't have done me any good now anyway.

"No I don't," he said, with panic in his eyes.

My instinct was to give him the ride for free. Well. To be honest, my instinct was to throw him out, but I was now two hours behind schedule etc., so I dug out all my starting change and handed him seventeen dollar bills.

Did he tip me?

I won't bore you with the answer.

After he scurried away, I drove down the block holding the twenty in my right hand, which was resting against the steering wheel at the one o'clock position. I glanced at Andrew Jackson's face. Ol' Andy Jackson, seventh president of the United States. A nun made us memorize the presidents back in sixth grade, so I knew our forefathers numerically. That was the only instance during my grade school years when I was good at math. But I had a secret. I didn't memorize the numbers, I memorized the words, i.e., "seven" rather than "7." Keep that under your hat. I wouldn't want my diploma repossessed.

Allow me to mention here that Andrew Jackson is not to be confused with Thomas "Stonewall" Jackson who commanded the rebs at Bull Run. I used to do that all the time. Not command rebs, but get confused.

Well, here I was once again unable to proceed with my life until I did something with money. I had a full tank of gas and a twenty-dollar bill in my hand, yet I couldn't pick up any fares until I had made small change out of the bill. O. Henry could have done wonders with that premise.

I drove past a car wash and slowed down because car washes have change machines. But then I stepped on the gas and kept driving. Just the thought of stuffing the twenty down the gullet of a machine that promised to give me change made me laugh out loud. I'm onto you, O. Henry.

Instead I drove to a Starbucks and bought a fresh cup of mocha. I'm not even going to apologize for that. I sure didn't apologize to the clerk for handing him a twenty at nine in the morning. I figured that a store that sells nothing but coffee would have plenty of change at nine in the morning. I'll admit it. I occasionally like to have a slug of yuppie mud with all its fancy frills. I'll take my alkaloid diuretics wherever I can get them. But I do prefer 7-11 joe. If there isn't a 7-11 in the vicinity, a Winchell's donut shop is Plan B. The joe at both places is almost indistinguishable, like the difference between Johnny Walker and Cutty Sark, but only cab drivers and hobos draw such fine distinctions.

It was nine-fifteen when I finally turned on my RMTC radio and started listening to the dispatcher yelling at the newbies. I did not head for a hotel. I normally park at the cabstand at the Brown Palace in downtown Denver at dawn and read paperbacks until a fare climbs into the backseat and says, "DIA." But that plan was down the crapper. I had to actually work that day.

This was what I meant when I said I knew I could easily make up a lost hour's worth of money. Jumping bells is how you do it. Taking calls off the radio is how a real cab driver makes money. He doesn't sit in front of hotels and he doesn't sit out at the airport. He takes radio calls one right after another. The fact that I'm a real cab driver does not invalidate the hypothesis. I know I'm a real cab driver because I have a license. I do sit in front of hotels but I never sit out at the airport. On the surface this might indicate that I am only half a real cab driver, or else half a phony. Take your pick. All I do know is that every April 15th I write "Taxi Driver" on my 1040 and not "Phony."

As I pulled away from the Starbucks I thought about opening up a mobile coffee shop. The idea was extremely appealing. I envisioned drivers stopped at red lights handing me money and taking pre-packaged cups of coffee out of my hand on their way to work. What coffee drinker wouldn't like to be able to reach through his window for a steaming cup of joe without having to stop at a 7-11 near the viaducts? The plan seemed so flawless that I knew I had better drive as fast as possible away from the unholy spot on the face of the earth where it had been conceived. I already had enough flawless plans to last a lifetime. Have I mentioned that I'm an unpublished novelist?

I listened to the calls being offered on the radio as I cruised. I was east of midtown, over by City Park. I wanted to stay away from the near occasion of hotels. I knew myself well enough to know that the sight of a vacant cabstand would instantly drain my vast reservoir of willpower. It's always good to know things about yourself even if most of it is gossip.

Then it came.

The Call.

CHAPTER 3

"Four thousand Cherry Creek Drive," the dispatcher said.

I snatched the mike and yelled, "One twenty-three!"

I heard dark laughter.

"Do you have enough change on you to break a one-hundred-dollar bill, Mister Tardy?" the dispatcher said. He was giving me the ol' one-two punch: a hundred-dollar bill plus a wisecrack. He knew I had just come on the road and that my ability to break a hundred was questionable.

"Check," I said.

"Okay, here's the deal," he said. "There's an elderly lady named Jacobs at a clinic who needs a ride to Capitol Hill, but she only has a one-hundred-dollar bill on her. So she wants us to send someone who will be able to break it for her."

"No problem," I said.

"It's all yours, Murph," he said, then he moved on down the road, offering bells and yells to newbies.

I hung up the mike and aimed my hood ornament at the Cherry Creek Shopping Center. The clinic was located nearby. A trip to Capitol Hill might amount to only eight dollars or so, even with a tip, but just the thought of seeing a one-hundred-dollar bill right at that moment did more to raise my spirits than a hot cup of alkaloids. I needed that sight.

I needed it bad.

Real bad.

I drove straight to Colorado Boulevard, turned right, and headed south. Traffic was light. I was breezing along. This was the stuff. I was an asphalt warrior headed into the fray. Things were back to normal. I spend an inordinate amount of time trying to get things back to normal. I don't know why. My normality is neither healthy nor realistic, but whatever it is, I'm good at it.

The clinic was located along the concrete-walled banks of Cherry Creek, the river where gold was discovered in the Denver area back in the 1850s. I'd like to give you an historical overview of the subsequent gold rush, but let's get to that elderly woman with the C-note burning a hole in her purse.

She was waiting outside the clinic. Short, white-haired, perhaps seventy years old, and wearing a print dress. Your basic garden-variety old lady. I could practically smell that eight bucks.

I pulled up at the front door and hopped out and hurried around and opened the right-rear door of my taxi.

She hobbled toward me. "Did the taxi company tell you about the one-hundred-dollar bill?" she said.

"Yes, ma'am."

"All right then," she said. I proceeded to help her into the backseat, which consisted of cupping her right elbow. I don't know how much help that was, but I was fishing for a tip.

I got back into the driver's seat and pulled away from the clinic. I had to make a run along the river before I could get my taxi turned around and aimed back toward Capitol Hill. Cherry Creek Drive runs one-way in opposite directions on either side of the river. It's complicated and annoying. Let's move on.

"My bank is located in the Cherry Creek Shopping Center, ma'am," I said. "We can stop there to break the hundred dollars. I'll even knock a dollar off the fare for you while you wait."

"Oh," she said. "I thought you would have the money on you."

"I'm just starting out for the day, ma'am, so I only have twenty dollars on me. But my bank is right on the way so we can just pull up to the drive-in and I'll get your one hundred changed. As I say, I'll give you a dollar discount on the cost of the ride."

I was talking to her image in my rear-view mirror. She nodded. She was silent for a moment. Then she said, "I have change at my house. If you would rather, we can just go to my house and I will get the money. I just didn't have anything smaller than a one-hundred-dollar bill on me and I was afraid a taxi driver wouldn't want to give me a ride if the money was at my house."

"Oh that's no problem," I said quickly.

Have I ever mentioned the fact that a lot of people seem to be afraid of cab drivers? They have this idea that we're something we're not, when in fact we are the complete opposite.

The old lady seemed to be one of those people. She obviously was afraid of the idea of getting into a taxi with no money on her person. I wish more people were like that. But I occasionally get people whose money is sitting in a house at the end of the ride. It's rare but not a problem. I've read that millionaires sometimes have to borrow money from friends when they're at lunch because they never carry hard cash on them, the pricks. Someday I hope to be a prick.

I drove to University Boulevard, bypassed my bank, and headed north toward "The Hill." Capitol Hill rises up from Lincoln Street in midtown and extends east across the city and out onto the plains, and stretches all the way across Kansas to the Mississippi River. I know what you're thinking—Capitol Hill is not a hill at all, and you're right. The truth is, Lincoln Street sits in a valley. I wish Albert Einstein was still alive. He would have a field day with that one.

I turned west at the intersection of 14th and University and drove the elderly woman seven or eight blocks and pulled around a corner and parked in front of her house. The house was on a rise. Six concrete vertical steps, then a short horizontal sidewalk, then six vertical steps. I helped her all the way up to the porch, which was horizontal.

"I'll be right back out with the money," she said.

She opened the screen door, opened the regular door, stepped inside, and shut both of them. I sat on the porch railing and waited. I felt kind of sad. I had really wanted to see ol' Ben Franklin's face. If you're like me, you rarely see hundred-dollar bills. It's like seeing a Picasso at the Denver Art Museum. You stare at it and think about how much money it's worth. Maybe you don't understand painting, and maybe you don't understand why something that looks like it could have been drawn by you is worth millions, but just knowing that armed guards are planted discreetly all around the room gives you an appreciation for art that you never got from Jon Nagy.

I glanced at my wristwatch. The woman had been gone five minutes. She was a slow walker it's true, but experience had taught me that people who are afraid of cab drivers are capable of performing feats of astounding strength in times of crisis, like lifting cars off trapped bodies. When I was a kid I always wanted to do that. Whenever I saw a man changing a flat tire, I kept my fingers crossed.

After ten minutes I went to the front door and tried to peek through the window. No-go. But I did not believe for one moment that she had run out on me. I'd had that happen. All cab drivers get a "runner" in the backseat sooner or later. It comes with the territory. You get skunked, and you feel skunked, but you rarely lose more than five or six bucks. Runners never seem to rack up the big meters. They're usually panic-stricken losers. Hell, if a guy gave me a good enough sob story I would give him a ride for free. I've done that, believe it or not. One time I pulled up in front of a house with a female fare in my backseat and she suddenly broke down crying, and said, "I don't want to go to jail." I was with her so far, but I didn't understand why she said it. "I don't have any money," she said. "I lost my job and my boyfriend. Please don't call the police."

That was a bona fide sob story, an authentic simon-pure tale of woe. She must have had me confused with a cab driver. She had no way of

knowing that I was an unpublished novelist and had about as much interest in calling the police as I ever do. I told her she didn't have to pay
me, that she could have the ride for free. The meter came to six bucks.
This may have been a big deal to her, but all I wanted was to get a new
fare into my backseat as quickly as possible. Then she leaned toward the
front seat and hugged my head. I wasn't going to mention that, but it
puts me in mind of even more colorful stories that I will never tell you.

I finally rang the doorbell.

It was another couple of minutes before I saw the silhouette of the
lady moving toward the door. She fiddled with the knob for a moment.
Apparently she had locked it behind her when she went in. I hadn't noticed that. I'm usually aware of it when people lock me out.

She dragged the door open and said, "You made me lose count!"

She was standing behind the screen door. I didn't know what to say.
Then she shoved the screen door open and stepped outside holding a
saucepan in her hand. The pan was filled to the brim with pennies.

"I was counting and the doorbell made me lose count!" she said.

I stared at the pot full of pennies. She had been counting out eight
hundred pennies. Part of my brain was wondering how high she had gotten, and the other part was helping me talk.

"I can't take pennies," I said.

Little-known fact—at least, it was little-known to me until I read
it in a newspaper article: pennies are not legal tender in America. This
is why people who try to pay their federal income taxes with jars of
pennies are told by IRS agents to go home and bring back real money.
That was in the article I read. The perpetrator was an anti-tax fanatic. I
felt bad for him. I always feel bad for optimists. I figure the Founding
Fathers had anticipated optimism, and wrote a law excluding the one-
cent piece as legal tender. You know a man has hit rock-bottom when
he devises a scheme to get the government's goat. Believe me, that goat
is ungettable.

"Why not!" she demanded. "What's wrong with pennies? It's perfectly good money!"

I stood there slack-jawed, flabbergasted, nonplused, and mute. Not only that, I was trying to calculate how long it would take to count eight hundred pennies with anything resembling accuracy. Included in this quick calculation were the recounts.

"Don't you have any dollar bills?" I said.

"This is my only money!" she said. "I have only pennies!"

If she had been fifty years younger I might have gotten rough. Instead I said, "Keep your pennies," and walked down the steps and got into my cab and drove away.

When I got to Colfax I said, "Jaysus!"

Normally I say "Fer the luvva Christ" but I was wound so tight that I went with Hemingway rather than Faulkner.

It was ten o'clock in the morning and I had earned three whole dollars. I turned west and drove six blocks before I remembered to turn on my RMTC radio. I didn't even know where I was going.

That "elderly lady" as I shall call her had completely destroyed my mental equilibrium. I couldn't get the image of that panful of pennies out of my mind. But what really bothered me was the fact that I had started thinking bad thoughts about an old lady—and liking it. I envisioned a couple of cops snapping the cuffs on her and snarling, "Save your sob story for the judge, granny."

I pulled into a 7-11 parking lot.

I turned off the engine and radio, and sat gazing at the glass storefront. The silence, and the sight of the ever-present "Help Wanted" sign on the door, had a calming effect. I felt like a penitent kneeling before a roadside shrine in Mexico.

After a few minutes I got out of my cab and went up to the door and peeked inside. No enemy in sight. I went inside, bought a cup of joe, came back out to my cab, got in, and sat sipping until my mental faculties were as intact as they ever get. Then I reached for the radio knob. It was at this precise point in time that I suddenly realized what had happened.

I had been the victim of a modus operandi!

The one-hundred-dollar bill. The panful of pennies. The print dress. It was all so obvious. The woman had done this before!

I heard dark laughter.

The radio was off so I knew the laughter was coming from inside my head.

I had been scammed.

That woman knew I would walk away in disgust without collecting the eight hundred pennies. That's what all the cab drivers had done after picking her up at the clinic, or the Safeway, or the AARP meeting— Rocky Cab, Yellow, Metro, Checker, all the cab companies. I was now a member of an exclusive club, an elite organization composed of taxi drivers who did not know each other's names and who would not recognize each other on the street. We had no secret handshake, password, discreet pin attached to our lapels, striped tie, raccoon hat, or inscribed ring that would indicate our membership in this fraternity of dupes. We shared only the unspoken bond of acute embarrassment.

How many of my fellow asphalt warriors had been skewered by Morgan La Fay?

Legions?

I didn't know.

I only knew that I would never speak of this thing to anyone as long as I possessed a taxi license.

It was a quarter after ten and I had three dollars to my name, although I had already spent at least that much on joe and Twinkies. But that was "yesterday's" money as I like to think, meaning part of my starting cash. As bad as I am at math, I am capable of mentally dividing numeric concepts into neat categories that make me feel like I'm not broke. I don't know why they teach algebra in high school when denial is far more useful.

I turned on the radio.

"Chambers and Arapahoe," the dispatcher said.

That was a million miles away in south Aurora, the suburb that runs along the eastern border of Denver. I sipped at my coffee and waited. I decided to remain at the 7-11 and listen for an address on Capitol Hill. I was afraid that if I started the engine I would black out and wake up in front of the Brown Palace with a paperback in my hand.

"Blood bank," the dispatcher said.

That was a call near the CU Medical Center over on Colorado Boulevard. Close, but not close enough. I was waiting for a bell on The Hill.

"They need cabs at Union Station!"

I chuckled softly. Only a newbie would make a dash for the railyards.

"Cherry Creek."

Interesting. There were no taxis at Cherry Creek Shopping Center. I had the urge to take the call, but I knew that by the time I got there another driver would have snatched the customer away. We cabbies have an old saying: "He who lives by the mall, dies by the mall."

The place is just too big and traffic is too heavy to expect a rich lady with a bag full of loot from Saks Fifth Avenue to stand on the sidewalk waiting for a taxi from the specific company that she had called. She'll flag down any cab that happens by. I'll admit it. I've "accidentally" picked up plenty of fares at the mall. Cherry Creek is a free-fire zone.

"Capitol Hill."

Did I mention the fact that my microphone was in my hand and my thumb was poised over the button? The dispatcher barely got the word "Capitol …" out before my thumb went into action CLICK "… Hill."

"One twenty-three," I said.

"Twelfth and Pearl."

"Check."

Bingo.

That's how it's done.

The address was three blocks away.

CHAPTER 4

It was an apartment building. I pulled up at the curb and waited. I have a rule-of-thumb when it comes to waiting. I call it "Four Minutes." Then I get out and walk all the way up to the front door—the entire distance—and ring the bell.

Four-and-a-half minutes later I was standing by a row of doorbell buttons looking for apartment #212. I pressed it, then stared at the speaker. I have the same attitude toward speakers as I have toward telephones. I hate talking to any machine—it's almost as bad as talking to people.

I pressed the bell again.

Then I walked back to my taxi and got in and radioed the dispatcher and told him I had a no-show.

"Hold on, Murph, we'll check it out," he said.

I almost told him not to bother. No-shows aren't that rare. The best thing to do is try and forget. Only newbies freak out about no-shows. Or perhaps I should say, newbies and drivers whose lives are disintegrating. I was furious. I waited for the dispatcher to make his call-back to the apartment.

"He's inside, Murph. He said he'll be right out."

"Check."

I shook my head with bafflement mixed with disgust. It appeared that I was about to encounter a person who had no fear of cab drivers.

I was right.

He looked about twenty-five years old. He came out of the building and waved to me, smiled, and climbed into the backseat.

"You sure got here fast," he said.

"I was only three blocks away when I took the call."

"Really? They told me it would take you twenty minutes to get here, so I hopped into the shower."

Holy cow.

This guy was a regular Spartacus.

I couldn't imagine anybody brave enough to call a taxi company and believe a word the dispatcher said.

"That's what they always tell the customers," I explained, as I started the engine and dropped my flag. "Sometimes it does take that long. Especially if we're real busy." My mouth was in the automatic-response mode. I was like a telephone answering machine. I had made this speech plenty of times. It bored me.

"Where ya headed?" I said.

"Glendale," he said. "The Ram."

A wave of pleasure swept through me. Glendale is a suburb east of Cherry Creek. It is sometimes referred to as Denver's "Youth Ghetto." In terms of residents it's sort of like Capitol Hill except all the young people in Glendale have money. Think of Benjamin Braddock in *The Graduate* living in a condo instead of a horrible apartment like mine. I do all the time.

"Do you work there?" I said as we pulled away.

"No, I'm meeting some friends. We're having a kind of informal high-school reunion. The official ten-year reunion is later this week, but my friends came in from out of town, so we're getting together for lunch."

This was far more information than I wanted. But at the same time it gave me plenty of material to pick through should I feel the need to chatter, which I didn't. But it did start me thinking about Blessed Virgin Catholic High School in Wichita, Kansas, where I had graduated in the late sixties. I held that against my fare. I had gone ninety-seven days without thinking about high school. Now I would have to start over at zero. I have never broken one hundred days and I doubt if I ever will. As soon as I get close to a hundred I start thinking about how close I am, and I have to start over.

On the other hand, I spend a lot of time thinking about the army, in the way that a defeated chess master replays a game in his head again and again, trying to figure out precisely where he went wrong, and considering the different moves he might have made in order to alter the outcome. Of course I would never tamper with the outcome of my two years in the army, which was a discharge. But it's the individual moves that keep coming back to me, the work-details I couldn't dodge, the officers who caught me saluting with my left hand, the promotions I never got, the demotions I deserved. No matter how many times I got away with goldbricking, malingering, or outright dereliction of duty, I was still haunted by the times I failed, which were like tiny flaws in an otherwise perfect diamond. Chess fascinates me.

The fare came to eight dollars. The kid gave me a ten and told me to keep it. I was amazed. In my experience young males never tip, but then I realized that since he was going to a ten-year reunion, he must be at least twenty-seven. Males tend to start learning the customs and traditions of tipping after they reach their "majority," which I define as the age of twenty-five. Anybody who doesn't tip after twenty-five is never going to tip, but I rarely encounter such men, and when I do I feel like an explorer who has stumbled across a heretofore unknown tribe deep in the jungle—but then one would hardly expect primitive people to adhere to the rigidly defined social customs that have evolved over thousands of years of civilization. H. Rider Haggard fascinates me.

"I'll need a cab in about an hour," the fine strapping young lad informed me.

"Give Rocky Cab a call," I said. "I might still be in the area."

I was skylarking of course. The odds of my ever being in Glendale again were zero. But I said it to make him feel good. It didn't cost me anything and anyway, there were plenty of desperate cabbies at Cherry Creek a mile away who would jump a bell at a bar called "The Ram." The Ram has a logo out front that looks like a snorting billy goat. It stands for manliness.

Just to make sure that I didn't get another youth in my cab, I drove south on Colorado Boulevard looking for a safe place to park and fill out my anemic trip-sheet. I pulled into the parking lot of a mattress store. I had chauffeured three people so far: Mister Twenty, the Madwoman of Chaillot, and a graduate of the playing fields of Eton. I had thirteen bucks to show for it. It was almost eleven o'clock in the morning. On an average Monday I would have grossed eighty dollars by now. My daily lease would have been paid off as well as my gas. Any other money I collected would have been all mine. Net profit. Pure gravy.

"Pure gravy," I said aloud as I set my trip-sheet aside and placed my pencil into my toolbox where I keep myriad other things that cab drivers need. I won't list them. Well ... here's a few: pliers, bandaids, toothpicks. That's enough. You get the idea.

"Puuuure gravy," I said as I turned on the Rocky radio, put the shift into gear, and pulled out onto Colorado Boulevard. I felt a song coming on. This is how it always happens. I don't know how John Lennon and Paul McCartney did it, but I usually do it following traumatic taxi experiences.

... Puuuure gravy, and it's mine all miiine ...

I was toying with various notes on the musical scale. Nothing nailed down of course. Again, I don't know how Lennon/McCartney did it, but I have always suspected that melody has more to do with hit songs than lyrics. I'm not very good in the melody department, but as an unpublished novelist I take pride in my lyrics, most of which you will never hear in their entirety. Like I always say, the First Amendment is not a license to shock schoolmarms.

"Chambers and Arapahoe," the dispatcher said.

This caught my attention. I wondered if it was the same Chambers and Arapahoe I'd heard earlier. I had to assume it was. The address was way, way east and way, way south. It made my mouth water. If I had been closer I would have grabbed the call, but the address was a million miles from Glendale, which is a good place to be.

Suburban calls are always intriguing though, because you expect the fares to be going to the airport. I don't know if I've mentioned this, but in general the only people who ever take cabs are the rich and the poor. The poor don't own cars and the rich never drive to the airport. The middle-class falls into neither of these categories. So when a call comes from a distant suburb, the ol' imagination gets fired up and you start envisioning someone from the bourgeoisie.

Let me add that while middle-class people rarely take cabs, when they do climb into your backseat they bring with them an attitude of wide-eyed wonder. In their minds they are experiencing the thrill of a guilty pleasure normally reserved for people who own Leer jets. Being a blasé man of the world myself, I tolerate their excitement with a condescending smile. I usually nab a buck tip.

"Five thousand East Mississippi."

I grabbed the mike.

"One twenty-three."

The address was less than a mile away. Burdens were being lifted from my shoulders like doves taking wing. My fortune was changing in the capricious way that fortunes always change, usually with the death of a rich relative. Suddenly I was getting decent calls from nearby locations. I was back in synch. I have said that you never win and you never lose in the taxi game, but by this I really mean that you win and you lose with a steadfastness that resembles the waves and troughs on a body of water. You win some and you lose some. It could be said that the wins and losses cancel each other, or you could say that everything balances out in the end. But no matter how hung-up you get on idioms, the IRS takes the same cut every year.

I drove to east Mississippi Avenue and pulled up in front of a large apartment complex. It was at the fringes of Glendale so I knew a young person would be coming out. I was right. She was perhaps twenty-two. She looked and was dressed like a fashion model. I won't waste your time or mine filling in the details. Just peek at a copy of *Cosmo*.

"I need to go to Dagwell's at Buckingham Square," she said.

I dropped my flag, turned on the meter, and began working my way over to Leetsdale Drive and on to Buckingham Square, a mall right across the border of Denver and Aurora. Leetsdale Drive is one of the few diagonal roads that cut across the Denver metro area. It was originally built by wagon trains. It links up with another pioneer trail called Parker Road, which continues on southeast to Texas or Oklahoma or some damn place. My knowledge of midwestern geography pretty much ends at Aurora. I know virtually nothing about Kansas, except that I grew up there.

I would have liked to chat with my fare, but fashion models do not like to engage in conversations with cab drivers. Fashion models are the exact opposite of me. But I knew she wasn't a fashion model. I knew exactly what she was. She was a sales clerk. She sold perfume or gloves or whatever wealthy women buy at Dagwell's, a posh boutique at the mall. One thing I had learned in my years of cab driving was that fashion models do not dress like fashion models when going to work. They are just like strippers. Sales clerks, on the other hand, do. Given the odds of my ever dating even one of those three categories of females, I'll take a sales clerk any day. I'm talking form over content, if you get my drift.

When I pulled up in front of Dagwell's, the fare came to nine dollars. I turned around in my seat—and my hair almost stood on end. The woman was writing a check.

Jaysus.

You can't spend checks. All you can do with a check is race to the fare's bank and try to cash it before it bounces. When I first started driving a cab I sometimes waited a week before depositing a check in my own bank, or going to the fare's bank to cash it, only to learn that the account was closed. I had learned my lesson, but ...

She handed me the check. I smiled and said thanks.

Call me spineless but I never argue with women. By that I mean I never win arguments with women.

I looked at the check. Her bank was in Glendale. I would have to drive right back there. I found this ironic. Statistically speaking, most of my problems that day involved either very old or very young women.

"Buckingham Square."

I grabbed the microphone.

"One twenty-three."

"Havana Bank."

Holy cow. The Havana Bank was right across the street. I tucked the check into my pocket, put the cab into gear, and forgot all about women.

It took me less than a minute to make my way across the intersection of Mississippi and Havana and pull up at the bank. I was beyond synch now. I was in The Zone. I sensed that all the hassles of the morning were nothing more than a trough. I was now riding the crest of a wave.

Two little old ladies came out of the bank. I mean that literally. They were old and they were little. They looked like characters out of Tolkien. I hopped out of the cab and opened the right-rear door and waited as they took forever to climb in.

When I got back into the driver's seat I looked back and said, "Where are you going?"

"Buckingham Square," one of them said.

"Buckingham Square?" I said.

"Yes."

"Do you mean the mall across the street?"

"Yes. We can't walk across the intersection. The lights change too fast."

My wave crashed to the beach. One minute later I opened the rear door and waited as they took forever to climb out. The meter came to one dollar and seventy cents, and that's exactly what they paid me. Just getting into a taxi costs a dollar-fifty, so the ride actually cost twenty cents. That was a record for me. After fourteen years I had finally hit rock-bottom.

I climbed into the driver's seat and started thinking about women again.

"Chambers and Arapahoe," the dispatcher said.

I ignored it. I was too busy thinking. It was almost noon and I had taken in fourteen dollars and seventy cents in legal tender. The check wasn't really "in the loop"—a phrase that I hate unless it's apt.

Then the dispatcher said, "Can I get anybody to take the Chambers and Arapahoe? I got some people trying to get to the airport."

Again, I ignored it. But it wasn't easy. I was now on the east side of town where the boulevards are broad and the red lights are few and far between and you can get from here to there quickly. But Chambers and Arapahoe was still a long ways off.

"Anybody?" the dispatcher said. "These people have been trying to get a taxi for the past hour. It's a DIA trip."

I had to admit that would be exceptionally decent money.

Reluctantly I reached toward the microphone, hoping that another driver would beat me to it. But he didn't, whoever he wasn't.

"One twenty-three. I'll take the Chambers."

"Thanks, Murph," the shadowy figure said. He gave me the address.

CHAPTER 5

N ow that I was committed, I began to comport myself as a professional. This is one of the drawbacks of commitment, and is the reason that I hate to get really good at anything.

I know what you're thinking—how many things is he good at? And you're right. But I am good at cab driving.

I cleared the decks, started the engine, pulled out onto Mississippi, and headed straight to Chambers Road. The road was wide and there was virtually no traffic. I'll confess. I was going approximately 8 mph over the speed limit. I'm not going to play games with you, unless you're a cop. I was making good time. I arrived at Chambers Road, which is way the hell east where farms still exist. I turned right and sped south. As I say, stoplights few and far between, and it's a big wide road. It's also hilly. The road goes up and down, up and down, like truly massive ocean waves in terms of breadth rather than height. You never seem to notice this where the landscape is full of condos, but out in the great wide open you can't miss those tidal swells.

"One twenty-three, I got a call-back. How soon, Murph?"

Damn.

"Ten minutes," I said.

This was an honest estimate. There are times in life when you have to be honest, which is often connected with the concept of being good at something. I feel like a fake when I wrestle that particular tag-team. Honesty and competence make my skin crawl. That's why I prefer hotels and paperbacks.

I stepped on the gas. There was no other traffic, although I did see some girls riding horses in a field. A blink and they were gone.

"How soon, Murph?"

Fer the luvva Christ.

"Five minutes."

I heaved a sigh of disgust. I had known since I passed Leetsdale Drive that I was eventually going to jump this bell. Why do I lie to myself when there are so many other people to lie to? If I had gone ahead and taken the bell when I knew I should have, I wouldn't be having a race with the devil.

A cluster of suburban homes appeared on the horizon. In my mind's eyes I was already there, a right turn, a left turn, and I would be pulling up at the house.

Then I was turning right a few blocks south of Arapahoe Road, and turning left into a cul-de-sac where a four-wheel drive vehicle was being loaded with suitcases. A group of people were standing around the jeepster tying down luggage on the roof with ropes. I slowed and pulled up alongside the group. A woman in her early sixties approached my window shaking her head no and saying, "We couldn't wait for you any longer so we asked our neighbor to drive us to the airport."

But I'm here.

I looked at the neighbor who was sitting in the driver's seat of his vehicle. He returned my gaze with a blank stare.

But I'm here.

"Could you please call the taxi company and tell them that we don't need you anymore?" the woman said.

But I'm here.

The passengers began climbing into their neighbor's vehicle.

I didn't answer the woman's superfluous question. She had no way of knowing that the only person who needed to be informed was me, and I had just been informed.

I took my foot off the brake and guided my cab around the cul-de-sac. I rolled back to the intersection and stopped at the crosswalk. I looked at my odometer and wondered how many miles I had racked up. I looked at my wristwatch. I looked at the rolling hills in front of me, looked at the smudge of smog on the horizon indicative of the city of Denver.

Here I am.

It seemed to me that I had seen something like this in the movies, but I couldn't remember which one. For some reason the image of the silent-film star Harry Langdon came to mind. He was staring at the camera and blinking. This was odd because on the inside I felt like Ben Turpin.

I drove back to Chambers and began heading north. There was no hurry now, but I still had to get back on the map before I could start playing the taxi game again. The ol' taxi game where you never win and ...

... and so on.

I glanced at my wristwatch, but I couldn't seem to read the hands. They were blurred by the image of fourteen dollars and seventy cents. I passed a telephone pole and noticed that it didn't have a shadow. This told me that it was high noon. I had learned in the Boy Scouts that when you're lost in the woods and don't know what time it is, just look at a telephone pole. It will tell you all you need to know about joining youth organizations.

Gas stations and suburban developments began to appear on the landscape. I had crossed the edge of the map and was back on the game board. If you don't like mixed metaphors, you're in the wrong taxi. So was I. The engine sputtered, and #123 began bucking strangely. I forgot all about my previous troubles and concentrated on this one. The last time I was in a taxi that began bucking strangely, I ended up standing by the side of the road watching the cab burn to a crisp. That was the same week I was hauled in by the police on suspicion of murder. Also kidnapping and robbery. The charges didn't stick. The guy wasn't even dead.

Then the engine died.

It came back to life.

I quickly scanned the horizon for a gas station. I wasn't going to risk another murder rap. I planned to pull off the road and park. I had learned my lesson, i.e., allowing your taxi to burn up can lead the police to think you're hiding something, and since I'm always hiding something I'd rather not have the law nosing around.

Fortunately I spotted a gas station at a far intersection. The cab was still lurching and losing power like everything else in my life, so I made a quick algebra calculation.

I waited until the (speed + distance) felt right, then I shifted into neutral and let the momentum (x) carry the cab (y) into the entrance of the gas station where I pulled up parallel to the border of the concrete apron. I stopped where a tow truck could easily back in and hook me up. I had no illusions about where this was headed. I wished I was as good with godsends as I was with disasters, but I didn't have as much experience.

I radioed the dispatcher and told him my cab had broken down. I gave him the address.

"The tow is on the way."

"Check."

I walked over to the gas station and entered the building. The decor was like that of a 7-11. Small compensation.

I used the restroom, then bought a soda and a Twinkie and walked back out to my lifeless pod. I got settled in the driver's seat, picked up a paperback, and began reading. Time passed. The tow truck showed up. The driver was the same man who had towed away Rocky Mountain Taxicab #127 when it burned up near the viaducts. He didn't recognize me. Small compensation.

The trip back to the motor took forever. I timed it. The driver dropped us both off in front of the garage. The mechanics came out wiping their greasy hands on rags, and popped the hood. I had a choice: stand around being useless, or go into the on-call room and tell Rollo I might need another taxi.

One of the mechanics walked over to the place in the parking lot where I had chosen to be useless. He held up the radiator cap.

"There wasn't any water in the radiator," he said.

"What?" I said. I wanted to say, "That's impossible," but like nuns, garage mechanics don't like to be contradicted.

"The cap wasn't screwed on tight. It almost fell off in my hand when I went to remove it. All the steam escaped. You're lucky the engine block didn't crack."

Call me Mister Vegas.

"Will I still be able to drive it?" I said.

"Yeah, as soon as we fill it with water."

He walked away.

I started to get nervous.

I rewound our conversation and played it back. By the time it ended I realized I was responsible for this minor calamity. It was confirmed when I went into the on-call room where Rollo informed me that I would have to pay the twenty-five dollar towing fee.

I didn't fight it. I knew the rules. I had seen other drivers try to fight it in the past, and Rollo had given them his standard speech: "Either you pay the fee, or you don't drive." He had two styles of saying this: loud or soft, depending on how much the driver's existence offended him.

I reached for my billfold just like a commonplace civilian. I dug into my "amateur" stash. The money I earn as a taxi driver is kept in a separate place, i.e., the pocket of my T-shirt. Even though I am no good at mathematics, I am quite capable of juggling abstract concepts that involve rectangles of paper. In high school I got A's in geometry. I was always good at figuring angles.

I handed Rollo the two twenties, and he handed me back fifteen dollars. This was a difficult and troubling time for me. My civilian cash had slopped over into my professional cash. I stood there for a moment looking at the remaining amateur fifteen dollars, and it occurred to me that if the two old ladies from *The Hobbit* had tipped me just thirty more cents I would have ended up grossing fifteen professional dollars for the day instead of fourteen dollars and seventy cents. I decided to place the fifteen dollars change into my T-shirt along with my fourteen-seventy. It would be like a loan from myself to myself. I figured this would have the effect of making me feel like I was doing okay for the day. But instead, my brain began to grow fuzzy. I kept thinking I was either back to zero for the day, or up thirty cents.

I hate algebra.

When I got back out to the garage, #123 was watered and ready to go back on the road. I thanked the guys in the garage, then climbed into the driver's seat and reached into my T-shirt and pulled out all of my money. I decided I either had twenty-nine dollars and seventy cents, or a minus thirty cents. I noticed that my hand was trembling. I quickly pulled out my billfold and put the amateur fifteen dollars back in. This had a calming effect. I now felt that I was mathematically on top of things. As a consequence I did something that I should not have done. I mentally tried to subtract fourteen dollars and seventy cents from twenty-five dollars.

Why I did it, I don't know.

You can carve that on my tombstone.

I might have continued trying to think, but fortunately my stomach growled and broke my lack of concentration. I started the engine and drove out of the lot. I headed for a MacDonald's. I normally buy my lunches at grocery store delicatessens, but I wasn't feeling very posh right then. I didn't even bother to turn on the radio and listen for calls. I decided I would just walk off the football field and wait for the brass ring to come around again. Sometimes a mixed metaphor is the only thing that keeps hope alive.

It was twelve-thirty in the afternoon when I popped the last French fry onto my tongue. I was parked in a slot at a MacDonald's on south Colorado Boulevard with the hood facing the street so I could watch the traffic roll by. I like to watch people doing things that I'm not doing. It reminds me that I don't have a foreman overseeing what I ought to be doing. For legal purposes, cab drivers are defined as "independent contractors." This means that when a driver is on the road he is his own boss, his own foreman, his own supervisor. He is also his own accountant, i.e., he does not have a secretary to handle his paycheck, calculate withholding and Social Security, etc. On the surface this might make cabbies appear to be actual grownups, but it doesn't always work out that way.

Instead of listening for calls on the radio, I just sat there chewing on fast food and watching the river of cars flow by.

… A river of caaaarrrs! …

I couldn't find a decent rhyme for cars. I tried "Mars" then gave up. I don't want to mislead you. Not all of the lyrics I compose are "finished products." They're like most of my novels.

I wadded up the wrappers and stuffed them into the hamburger sack. I grabbed the Twinkie wrappers and empty soda cans, then got out of my cab and walked across the parking lot to a trash barrel and tossed everything. This bit of policing-up gave me the delusion that I had things under control. On the way back to my cab it occurred to me that my Maw used to clean our house in Wichita all day long. I wondered if …

But no. Nobody would expend that much furious energy maintaining a delusion.

Would she?

I was my mother's son though, and I had spent the past twenty-seven years living like I do now. On top of that, I had been hugging to my breast the delusion that someday I would write a best-selling novel. That's a long time to hug anything. So I had at least two delusions that I knew of—my real life, and my dream life. That appeared to cover everything.

But I wondered if there was a third "something" that lay between reality and fantasy that I could screw up. I mean I knew I could screw it up, but did it exist?

There must have been some magic in that ol' fast food that day, because after I climbed into the driver's seat an idea occurred to me. I reached into my jeans pocket and pulled out thirty cents. It was change from the Whopper—excuse me—Big Mac. I reached up and tucked the three dimes into my T-shirt pocket. I now had exactly fifteen dollars in my professional stash. But this was not to be construed as a loan from myself to myself. It was a cry for help.

CHAPTER 6

L et me explain.

Whenever I get a passenger in my backseat who has a serious personal problem, I try not to get involved. Or perhaps I should say, I pretend that I'm not going to get involved in his or her personal life. Ultimately I do though, and sometimes I live to regret it, and sometimes I don't. If things work out well, I regret it, because it only encourages me. However, this was the first time I had ever tried to get personally involved in my own life.

I told myself not to think of the thirty cents as a loan, but rather, think of it as three pennies. By this I meant the sorts of pennies you see in a cup next to a café cash register, pennies that can be freely used if a customer comes up short. Customers can also toss extra pennies into the cup if they don't want to carry them. The thing is, Americans neither want nor like pennies, and would rather see coinage stop at the nickel level. But the government makes us have them because when you live in a country of three hundred million people, three hundred million pennies equal three million dollars that can be taxed by the IRS—and that's just one penny.

Let's take it up to four pennies. That's twelve hundred million pennies, or twelve million dollars. And that involves just one single transaction. Now suppose three hundred million people transact a half-dozen exchanges of pennies per day. Of course there are factors that affect the sum total—like for instance, babies never go out for coffee.

But even if we cut the sum in half it still turns out to be a big chunk of tax money. Now, when you multiply this river of copper going into the treasury three-hundred-and-sixty-five times a year … well … I can't multiply that high mentally or with a pencil, although I would be willing to give it a shot with a Texas Instrument or even a spreadsheet as soon as I learn how to use spreadsheets. But my point is, instead of fourteen dollars and seventy cents, "Voila, you now have fifteen dollars!" I said out loud.

I sat there listening to myself. I had never been on the receiving end of my own logic, or advice, or whatever I do behind a steering wheel, so I almost felt a moral imperative to get into the backseat.

But now that I had an even fifteen dollars in my pocket, I was suddenly able to see everything clearly. I needed to gross one-hundred-and-thirty dollars in order to go home with a fifty-dollar profit. With my $70 lease, $10 gas, and $25 tow cost, I was already minus $105 for the day. But I had earned fifteen dollars in cash, which brought me to minus $90. Plus, I did have a check for ten dollars in my pocket. So if I cashed that, I would be minus $80.

It was one o'clock in the afternoon and I had six hours left on my shift. Six hours to earn eighty bucks. That would bring me up to zero. After I hit zero, everything I grossed would be pure gravy.

"Puuuure gravy," I said, as I started the engine.

Any cab driver who can't rake in at least fifteen dollars an hour has no right to call himself an asphalt warrior. That's what I told myself as I raced toward Glendale. I never thought I would be back in Glendale, but that's where the sales clerk's bank was located. My original plan had been to go to my own bank at Cherry Creek and drop off the check and try to forget it. Let my bank discover the sales clerk's account had been closed two weeks ago. I didn't want to find out from my bank. It gets old.

But things were different now. I was riding in the backseat, and the driver was advising me to go to her bank and cash the check, bite the bullet, get back up on the horse, and take charge of my life for the next ten minutes. I was relieved to have someone else telling me what to do.

Of course, part of this willingness to listen to my own advice was based on the fact that if things didn't work out, I couldn't be blamed. Instead, I could blame myself.

I know what you're thinking—what a weasel. Can't accept personal responsibility. But I was depressed by the knowledge that if I didn't net my standard fifty bucks I would be driving on Tuesday, which is my standard day off—along with Thursday, and Saturday, and Sunday. But I was looking for a scapegoat, and I happened to be handy.

Most of the people I help are as depressed as I was that day. I don't want to come off like some kind of nickel psychologist, but there seems to be a causal link between problems and depression. That's just a layman's observation though.

The Glendale Bank & Trust was on the east side of Colorado Boulevard. I pulled into the lot and parked, got out, and tried not to hurry into the lobby. People who look like me should never hurry into or out of banks. "Moderation in everything," said Willie Sutton.

There were twelve teller cages, and exactly one teller working. Five people were ahead of me. I felt like I was in the post office, whereas in reality I was in The Land That Forward Motion Forgot. Not that it mattered. I was busy concentrating on looking like a decent human being. One of the ways I do this is to stand at attention—shoulders back, stomach in, chest out, head erect, eyes level. They tried to teach me this in the army but I never got the "stomach in" part right. I knew the theory though, and was able to fake it in the bank. After all, I was among civilians.

I finally got up to the teller and said, "I would like to cash this check."

By "like" I meant "enjoy" rather than "desire." To successfully cash a fare's check for once would make me truly happy. My desire was as irrelevant as ever. But I doubt if the clerk caught my subtle shade of meaning. People rarely do. It's gotten me into trouble a time or two.

Anyway, if you think standing in line at a bank is an adventure in stasis, try cashing a check that might be made of rubber. There's a moment when the earth ceases to rotate, and all the air disappears. You feel like Keir Dullea after the explosive bolts went to work.

"Here you are, sir," the clerk said. The clerk was a woman, by the way, but I deliberately try to avoid making distinctions between men and women when I'm not at Sweeney's Tavern. What's the point?

"Thank you," I said, and I meant it.

I turned around and almost careened into the latest arrivals in line.

"Excuse me," I said to a short man in a gray suit. The words "Willy Loman" came to mind. This happens to my mind a lot.

I strolled out of the bank with a ten-dollar bill in my hand. I got seated inside 123 and pulled my cash out of my T-shirt pocket. I had a ten-dollar bill, another ten, four one-dollar bills, and one dollar in coins. I set the tens in a stack on the lid of my plastic briefcase, the fives in another stack, and the coins in a neat tower. Then slowly and carefully I removed my billfold from my back pocket, opened it, withdrew a dollar, and lay it down on the seat beside the briefcase.

I carefully picked up all the change and put it into my T-shirt pocket. I started to lose focus, but I did my best to maintain. I picked up the dollar bill from the seat and carefully set it on the stack of four ones, so that I now had five ones.

"Two tens and five ones," I said aloud, my eyes flitting back and forth at the rectangles. I wanted to make double sure I was doing this right. Triple sure even. In fact, I lost count of how many times I counted to make sure I wasn't screwing this up. If you think I have been kidding about being numerically challenged, I submit all of the above as evidence.

I finally took the last big step. Again, it was like the moment in *2001* when Keir fired himself from the pod into the airlock—do or die, pal.

I reached into my shirt pocket, withdrew the change, and shoved it into my jeans pocket.

Point Of No Return.

I was now down eighty bucks.

I breathed a sigh of relief. I decided I would drop by my apartment and grab some more amateur cash. I don't like walking around half-broke. That's a young man's game. But don't let me mislead you. I wasn't impoverished. I did possess an adequate amount of life-survival money. I had it in my bank, and I had it hidden in various books at home. But on that day I knew that if I used my taxi earnings to buy even one Twinkie, the universe would implode.

Someone tapped on my shotgun window. I looked around. Willy Loman was peering in at me. He was holding a briefcase. "Can you give me a lift back to my office?"

"Hop in," I said, hoping he was indulging in a subtle shade of meaning, since I translated "lift" to mean "hire for pay."

I immediately dropped my flag and turned on the meter.

"Where to?" I said.

"It's only about six blocks," he said, "but I'm on my lunch hour and I'm running late. I don't quite feel up to walking that far that fast."

He didn't look like he could walk that far at all. I had seen both Lee J. Cobb and Dustin Hoffman perform the role of Willy Loman, and this guy was more of the Dustin type. Lee J. Cobb was good in the role, but he had struck me as a little too physically robust to play a broken-down loser. I thought he was better cast as the crazed juror in *12 Angry Men* who was determined to send a teenaged murder suspect to the electric chair based on flimsy evidence. That's my kind of Lee J. Cobb.

I drove out of the lot. Six blocks. Three blocks more than my first fare of the day, Mister Twenty.

A minute or so later I pulled up at the curb. Willy gave me a five-dollar bill and told me to keep the change.

"Thanks," I said, and I meant it. I was Mister Kiss-ass that afternoon. I was thanking everybody who would stand still.

I pulled away from the curb and drove north on Colorado Boulevard. I was now at minus $75. I headed over to the heart of Capitol Hill, my home ground. It always makes me feel good to jump bells in the vicinity of my crow's nest. It makes me feel like I'm just pretending to work and can go home any time I feel like it, which is technically true, but I try not to think about that. You don't want to give guys like me ideas.

I sometimes dream I'm driving a taxi that I did not lease. In this dream I go to Rocky Cab, climb into a vacant taxi, and drive away. I cruise around Capitol Hill. I pick people up and let them off and take their money. If it wasn't for the Public Utilities Commission, I could actually do that in my '64 Chevy, assuming people would climb in. I wonder who the first taxi driver in America was.

Anyway, I drove up to 13th Avenue, turned west, and headed toward home. I knew I could earn more than fifteen dollars an hour working The Hill. The Hill is as active as an anthill, which is why I normally avoid it. Again—hotels and paperbacks. If I wanted to work, I'd get a real job.

I cruised down 13th and pulled into the dirt parking lot behind my apartment building. I got out and climbed the fire escape. It felt weird to be climbing my fire escape on a Monday afternoon when I was supposed to be at work. I paused halfway up the steps and looked around. I nodded. Everything looked the same as it did on Tuesday afternoon when I made my weekly shopping trip. I include going to the laundry or even to the gas station as "shopping." If I leave my apartment and come back with less money, it goes into the category of "shopping." Simplify—that's my motto. I have quite a few mottoes. I ought to whittle them down to a manageable number.

I entered my apartment. I felt like a burglar. Again, it was Monday. I bypassed my bookshelf where I keep my daily cab profits. I keep profits in a copy of *Lolita*. I used to keep them in *Finnegans Wake* but it weighs too much. I got tired of lifting it off the shelf three times a week. I keep my shopping money in a copy of the *New American Bible*, which sits on a bookshelf in my bedroom alongside a number of high school textbooks, including algebra and Latin. The textbooks are a kind of camouflage.

Maybe it's because I was raised Catholic but I've always felt that no burglar would ever steal a Bible during a heist, but if he did, it would have to be the King James version with gold trim and lots of colored bookmarks. That's why I keep a *New American Bible* on my shelf. I figure anyone who would sink low enough to steal a Bible wouldn't touch a version with all the "thees" and "thous" updated to "you."

And as an English major and an aspiring novelist I always felt it was proper and necessary to have read the Bible, the oldest and most profound book known to Western Man. Okay. I'll admit it. I couldn't get through the King James. Too many thees and thous. But then I didn't want to steal it, I wanted to read it. That's why I bought the American version, so I could grasp the content. W.H. Auden once said, "Thou shalt not read the Bible for its prose." But in fact, I have read the Bible for its prose. I like to read selections from "The Song of Solomon." Afterward I ask myself, "How did people write so good in the olden days when people today write so crummy?"

I went into the bedroom and opened the Bible to "The Song of Solomon" where I keep my civilian money. The money actually goes into *Lolita* first, then later I transfer it to the Bible, then I deposit it in the bank. *Lolita,* Bible, bank. Sounds like the plot of *Elmer Gantry.* I categorize going to the bank as "shopping," too. Even when I'm sitting on a barstool at Sweeney's I'm shopping. I shop until I drop.

I took out two twenties and added it to the "damaged" fifteen in my billfold. I put the Bible back on the shelf and pressed the algebra and Latin books against it, as well as a Spanish textbook and an earth science textbook. Anybody who wanted to steal my cash would have to plow through my junior year of high school.

I now had fifty-five dollars worth of civilian money in my billfold, and fifteen taxi-bucks in my shirt pocket. This gave me the delusion that I had already netted my fifty dollars for the day, while at the same time it made me feel like a phony. I was my old self again.

I glanced at my wristwatch as I walked back through the living room. One-thirty. I had five-and-a-half hours left on my shift. Instead of feeling desperate, which would have been logical, I felt like a football quarterback. My team was behind six points with five-and-a-half minutes left in the game. You might wonder what the six-point figure is analogous to in terms of cab driving, but I just made it up. "You need a touchdown and a field-goal, bub. Now get out there and show the world what the fighting Irish are made of!"

I closed my crow's nest and sauntered down the fire escape with the aplomb of the captain of a high school football team who knows he's going to cop the nomination for homecoming king. I never played football in high school, or went to a homecoming dance. Those jocks were insufferable. Again, let's move on.

I climbed into 123, backed around, and pulled onto 13th Avenue. I aimed the grill at midtown and turned on the Rocky radio to start taking calls.

"One twenty-three, pick up."

I was astonished. As soon as the radio came on I heard myself being paged.

"One twenty-three, pick up."

I plucked the microphone from its hook on the dashboard, but before I got the button pushed I heard sirens. I saw a flash of red lights in my rear-view mirror. I took a moment to slow and pull over to the curb before raising the mike to my lips, but then I paused as three cop cars raced up behind me. Two of them stopped, and the third one swung around in front of me and blocked my path.

I was boxed in.

"Get out of the taxi!"

"One twenty-three, pick up."

"Get … out … of … the … taxi!"

"One twenty-three, pick up."

Cops were crouching behind their cars aiming their guns at me.

"Put down the microphone, Murph," someone said. It was me. I looked in the rear-view mirror. The backseat was empty. Apparently I was in the front seat.

"Let go of the microphone and raise your hands," I said.

I quickly complied.

The mike bounced off the floor. I had seen enough cop shows to know how to raise my hands. Elbows positioned at ninety-degree angles. Fingers spread. Head erect. Wait for further instructions.

CHAPTER 7

I found myself "kissing the asphalt" that afternoon. But let's back up thirty seconds.

"Get out of the taxi with your hands up!" a cop shouted.

To do this I had to lower my left hand below the windowsill. I had seen criminals do this on TV and to me it always looked like they were going for a gun. I wondered what it looked like to cops. Just to make sure it didn't look like anything, I did it real slow. I don't know if that's grammatically correct, but it got the job done. I kept my right hand in the upright position while I eased the door open with my left and proceeded to extricate my body from the driver's seat—again, real slow.

"Lay face-down on the ground! Hands behind your head!"

Correct grammar was back "in the loop" so I hurriedly complied. I gazed directly at the asphalt. I wanted the police to understand that I was going to fully cooperate, and I did this by lying perfectly still. This was body language for "silence." I was golden.

I heard running footsteps, doors opening, puffing and grunting, and low voices. I also heard the clicks and static sounds of police radios. They were talking to headquarters, I assumed. This was one of the few times in my life where I felt it didn't really matter if I made an erroneous assumption. I idly wondered if police dispatchers ever yelled at newbie cops.

Throughout all this, I kept hearing my dispatcher saying, "One twenty-three, pick up. One twenty-three, pick up." But after awhile it stopped.

More cop cars arrived. I knew because I peeked.

A finger tapped my shoulder. "Are you the driver of this taxi?"

"Yes, sir."

"What's your name?"

"Murph."

"Full name?"

"Yes."

"What's your full name?"

"Oh ... Brendan Murphy."

I tend to forget that. The police never seem to though.

"All right, you can stand up."

It hurt my knees to kneel on the asphalt before hoisting my beer belly erect. To be honest, I rarely kneel.

Five cops cars were blocking the street now. Traffic was being diverted down side streets. Red lights were still flashing. Police officers were roaming around my taxi. The doors to 123 were wide open. A nearby cop was talking into a radio attached to his upper body. His head was bowed a bit as if he was telling secrets to his shoulder.

"Mr. Murphy, would you please step over to the sidewalk with me?" the policeman said.

I followed him onto the curb and across a six-foot stretch of dirt to a flagstone sidewalk. A lot of the sidewalks on Capitol Hill are made of flagstone. They're from the cowboy days.

"I'll have to ask you to wait here," he said. "We have some people who want to talk to you."

"All right."

I thought the cop would walk away, trusting me not to bolt. But he didn't do either. He stood right next to me while the other policemen prowled around my taxi.

An unmarked car cruised up to the scene of the ... well, not "crime," but just the place where we were. Two men in gray flannel suits climbed out. I started to blanch, but then I stopped. For one moment I thought

I recognized them. I thought they were two cops that I had a passing acquaintance with: Detectives Duncan and Argyle. But these were different detectives. I could tell they were detectives by the way the other policemen crowded around and began talking fast. Cops don't talk that way to rubberneckers. They do it only to men who have years of experience tucked under their belts, along with pistols.

I knew not to ask the uniformed policeman questions. Duncan and Argyle had taught this to me, although not on purpose. It was a learned thing. I didn't know what was going on, but I did know one thing: they would tell me. They always told me. Sometimes down at police headquarters.

The two detectives walked toward me. Except for their faces, they looked just like Duncan and Argyle.

"Is your name Brendan Murphy?" one of them said.

"Yes, sir."

"Are you the driver of this taxicab?"

"Yes, sir."

"My name is Detective Ottman. This is my partner, Detective Quigg. We're with the Robbery Division of the Denver Police Department."

I immediately wondered if Detective Quigg was related to Mayor Quigg Newton. Quigg Newton was the mayor of Denver in the late forties. He and Bob Hope once owned the Channel 4 TV station. I learned this in a Denver history class in college. You learn all kinds of things in college. I recommend college to anybody who doesn't know much.

"I need to ask you a few questions," Ottman said.

"Okay."

"Mr. Murphy, did you pick up a fare from the Glendale Bank on Colorado Boulevard sometime during the past thirty minutes."

"No," I said.

He raised his chin and looked sort of "down" at me, even though we were about the same height. He was acting as if he didn't believe me.

"Wait. Well. Yes," I said.

He lowered his chin. "Is it no or yes?" he said.

"It is yes. But I didn't pick up a fare from the bank. I mean, I was parked in the lot at the bank, and a man tapped on my window. He asked if I could give him a lift."

"You were in the parking lot of the bank?"

"Yes I was. But …" I stopped.

"But what?"

"What I mean is, he didn't call for a cab from the bank. I just picked him up off the street. He was what I call a 'pedestrian'."

Ottman nodded.

"Could you describe the man to us?"

"Yes."

"Go ahead."

"He looked like Willy Loman."

"What do you mean?"

"He was nondescript."

"How so?"

"He had the kind of face and demeanor that wouldn't stand out in a crowd. In fact, I saw him twice."

"Where did you see him the first time?"

"In a crowd. He was standing behind me in line at the Glendale Bank."

"So you were *in* the bank."

I heard those italics. They pulled me up short. People often use italics when they think they have caught me in a lie. Nuns taught me this.

"Yes. I was in the bank cashing a check, and when I turned to leave I almost bumped into the man. After I got outside to my taxi, he came out and asked if I could take him down the road."

"Down the road? Did he say that?"

"No. That's cabbie lingo. He said he needed to go six blocks."

"Mister Murphy, I'm afraid we're going to have to ask you to come down to headquarters and make a written witness statement. I know this is going to inconvenience you. It may take awhile. I can't guarantee that you'll be able to drive your cab again today. We just spoke with your supervisor, Mister Hogan. He knows that we have been looking for you and that you are all right. But you might want to contact him and let him know what's happening."

"Okay. But I have one problem."

"What's that?"

"I don't know what's happening."

"Didn't anybody tell you?"

"No."

"For the love of Christ," Ottman muttered under his breath.

I liked that. I wondered if "Ottman" was an Irish name. It sounded sort of Turkish.

"The man who was in your backseat is suspected of robbing the Glendale Bank & Trust."

I nodded. By then I had come to that conclusion on my own, only I was hoping I was wrong. I rarely hope, but when I do, I'm usually wrong.

I went back to 123, reached in and picked up the mike from the floor. I switched the transmitter over to Channel 4, the private line used for matters not relating to bells. I told the dispatcher that I would be off-duty for the next hour or so, and that I wasn't certain if I would be back on the road today. He said he would pass the message along to Hogan. I hung up the mike and walked away from the cab.

I looked at my wristwatch. I did this blatantly so the cops would not see me doing it surreptitiously, which was what I wanted to do. I don't like people to know that I know what time it is. It was two o'clock. My day was now officially shot to hell.

It was true that if I finished with this police business by three o'clock and got back on the road, there was the slimmest possibility that I could drive until seven and get back to zero. I was down seventy-five bucks. Then I realized that five of my gross had come from the bank robber. Maybe I was carrying stolen money. I wondered if I should tell this to Ottman and Quigg. Maybe the money was "marked" and if I tried to spend it, bells and whistles would go off at Langley.

I decided to come clean.

But I didn't come clean right then. I was going to wait until I was writing my witness statement at headquarters. I wondered if Duncan and Argyle were working that day. If so, I felt I ought to make a special point of not dropping in on them.

A patrolman in a black-and-white drove me to police headquarters in downtown Denver. We entered through the basement parking lot. I had been there before. That was the time I was suspected of murdering a homeless man. When I was suspected of kidnapping that eighteen-year-old girl I had not been brought to HQ. So far the police had brought me in for kidnapping, assault, and murder, and now I had a bank robbery to write home to Maw about.

I was escorted into a large room. It was different from the small room where I had been "grilled" about the murder. Since I wasn't a suspect, they were giving me wagon-room, although I noticed that the door clicked with a suspicious locking sound when the cop left me alone.

He had given me a pen and a copy of an official police witness-statement form. I immediately became worried that I would screw it up and have to ask for another form and start over. "Know thyself," said someone who didn't even know me. The first sheet of paper was pre-printed, but I had been given extra sheets of blank typing paper. The cop had told me to use as many sheets as I needed.

I held the pen poised over the official sheet. It was like holding my fingers poised over the keys of a typewriter. I didn't know where to start. I had never written autobiographical fiction before, and I sure didn't want to start now. Most of my novels are pure fantasy, especially the part about selling them. I don't believe in writing the kinds of books produced by, for instance, Jack Kerouac, which were virtual diaries. If I ever revealed the things I actually did during my travels around America, my only readers would be bounty hunters. I am more into writing what I call the "Jules Verne genre," i.e., sci-fi, fantasy, horror, etc. In other words, things I know absolutely nothing about.

But that wasn't the problem now. The problem was trying to figure out the precise point at which my involvement in this mess began. Birth came to mind. Then I realized Detective Ottman had given me a lead-in: the first time I saw Willy Loman. Not the real Willy Loman, who was fictional, but the fake one who was real, i.e., the man in the bank.

I started out by asking myself why I had been at the bank. A sales clerk at Dagwell's had given me a check. Should I mention her? Things could get interesting if she got roped into this case. I wouldn't mind catching her eye across a crowded courtroom.

I began writing.

"At one o'clock this afternoon, I, Brendan Murphy, a legally licensed driver for the Rocky Mountain Taxicab Company ..."

I stopped writing. It sounded like the title of a book about a man going to the electric chair:

I, Brendan Murphy

My shoulders drooped. I started writing again, telling the cops everything I had done from the moment I pulled up at the Glendale Bank until the moment I started "kissing the asphalt." I didn't write that down, but I wanted to. I thought the cops might take note of my lyrical prose imagery and ask if I had any aspirations to become a novelist. Maybe some flatfoot could put me in touch with an agent.

After I finished, I signed the statement.

Well, that was that. I set the pen aside and waited for the officer to return. He arrived thirty seconds later, which indicated to me that the police were watching on a closed-circuit TV. But I had suspected that all along. Whenever I'm anywhere, I think people are watching me. I could be locked inside a safe at the bottom of the Marianas Trench, and I would still comport myself like a gentleman.

"Is that everything, sir, or am I now free to leave?" I said politely.

"Detectives Ottman and Quigg still need to speak with you," the cop said, and he walked out of the room with my statement in his hand.

CLICK.

Went the door.

I folded my arms and leaned against the back of the chair. But I quickly unfolded my arms. I was afraid it might have made me look surly. I speak fluent body language, so I knew what I was doing. When you drive a taxi you have to be able to read what I call "the grammar of the flesh and the syntax of the bones." What people do is often more significant than what they say, especially when they're getting positioned to shove the back door open and take off running without paying.

My rear-view mirror serves as my textbook.

CHAPTER 8

The door opened. Detectives Ottman and Quigg walked in. I sat perfectly still. But I wasn't fooling myself. Cops are also students of body language. So are bartenders. I've never actually made a complete list of body-speakers. I include here only the students I know best.

"We read your statement," Detective Quigg said. "It was pretty thorough, but we have one question."

"Yes, sir?"

"You indicated that you dropped the man off near a parking lot. Did you see him go into his office?"

"No I didn't."

"Did he say where he actually worked?"

"No, sir."

Quigg nodded.

I felt like a failure.

Even though I rarely make assumptions, I now had to assume that the bank robber did not actually work at an office. I mean, why would someone who stole money have a job?

"Can I ask you something?" I said.

"Certainly, Mr. Murphy."

"How much money did he steal?"

"Well … we're not at liberty to talk about that, Mr. Murphy, but I will say that he got a large amount."

I nodded. Then I looked Detective Quigg right in the eye. "Did he use a gun?"

Quigg nodded.

"Can I assume he had the gun with him when he got into my cab."

Quigg nodded.

I sat there looking at the two detectives, and I felt my face beginning to grow warm. My cheeks were tingling.

"Are you all right, Mr. Murphy?" Ottman said.

"Yes."

"Would you like a glass of water?"

"No."

"Your face is turning red," he said.

"I know," I said. But it wasn't embarrassment. It was something worse. It was reality.

All of a sudden I was back in my taxi with a man sitting behind me with a gun. But here's the strange part: it was as if my skin was thinking about this, and not my brain. My flesh felt like it was starting to flip out.

"Get him a glass of water," Ottman said, and Quigg left the room. He came back a minute later with a paper cup filled with ice-cold water. I drank it. My cheeks cooled down. I felt then that I understood what was going on. My brain was refusing to extrapolate, i.e., refusing to think about the existence of a gun, and as a consequence my blood was pooling on the surface of my skin rather than entering my cerebral cortex. I was undergoing a "jugular log-jam," which was exactly what I wanted.

"Will you need me for anything else today?" I said, my voice rather thin.

Ottman shook his head no. "We will probably be getting in touch with you again. We're talking to a number of witnesses."

"I guess you haven't caught the guy, huh?" I said.

"No we haven't, Mr. Murphy. But I will tell you there is a city-wide search going on right now."

I nodded. The nod is a handy piece of body language that usually means absolutely nothing, although it can be translated in a number of ways, such as "Yes," or "I understand," or "The End," which was what I was saying there. I wanted to leave.

"Are you finished with me?" I said.

"Yes," Quigg said. "You can leave. That's all."

I wanted to ask if they had found any fingerprints in my cab, but I didn't. I had seen enough cop shows to know not to ask a million questions about a case that was currently under investigation and was none of my business. I wasn't a journalist.

As I walked out of the room it occurred to me that instead of writing "The End" at the end of my novels, I should write, "That's All." It could become my personal trademark, like e.e. cummings and his lowercase gimmick. You think irrelevant thoughts when you're suffering from a jugular log-jam. I read somewhere that the human brain can't live for more than three minutes without a fresh supply of circulated blood. Sensitive bastard.

The same patrolman who had driven me to HQ chauffeured me back to the location on 13th Avenue where my taxi was parked. There was another black-and-white unit parked behind my cab. I thanked my driver before I climbed out. He smiled and nodded. I hardly ever see cops smile. I don't know why I bring that up.

I opened the door to 123 and climbed in. The two police cruisers rolled away. After they disappeared from view it was as if nothing at all had happened. It was as if I was simply parked at the curb waiting for a fare to come out of an apartment building. I was barely a block away from my crow's nest, and all of a sudden I wanted to drive home and go to sleep.

Instead, I dialed Channel 4 and told the dispatcher that I was bringing my cab back to the motor. He said he would tell Hogan. I switched over to Channel 1 in time to hear the dispatcher yell at a newbie. I left the radio on all the way back to Rocky Cab. There's an unwritten rule at Rocky Cab that says a driver should leave his radio on at all times for safety's sake, and I had not obeyed that non-rule that day. I practically never obeyed it. Usually I turned on the radio at a whim. Another reason for leaving the radio on is to listen for bells. That's why they give you a radio, so you can take calls.

Let me explain:

We drivers know that the cab company doesn't really like it when we sit at the cabstands or loaf at the airport, even though both places are legitimate locations to pick up fares. They want us to take calls off the radio, to drive around and service customers, and thus increase business. Drivers who loaf at DIA are called "airport rats" by the drivers who don't loaf at DIA. I was an airport rat when Stapleton Airport was in business before DIA was built. I didn't care what anybody called me. I made my fifty bucks a day and went home. After DIA opened, it became impossible to make my nut, so I moved my loafquarters to the cabstands in downtown Denver. And I didn't turn the radio on. I read paperbacks and waited for fares to come out of the hotels. And when they got in and said, "DIA," I took them to the airport with my radio off. I almost never turned my radio on because I almost never jumped bells, because I wanted as few people in my cab as possible during a shift. I just wanted to be left alone, make my fifty, and go home.

But I listened to the radio all the way to the motor, and after I got there I turned it off and tried not to think about what would have happened if the radio had been on while I was driving the robber away from the bank. But I knew what would have happened. The dispatcher would have transmitted a code word to let all the cab drivers know that one of us was in jeopardy. Transmission of bells would have ceased. There would have been other verbal signals given by the dispatcher to indicate that all taxis were on radio lockdown and that we drivers should be wary of any passengers in our backseats.

This was what I meant by "reality."

My method of dealing with reality has always been denial. By not listening to my radio, I was always denying the reality of the danger of cab driving. But it's like I've often said: I need some kind of goddamn therapy.

I gathered my things and got out of 123, walked across the lot and entered the on-call room. Rollo was seated inside the cage. He wasn't eating a donut. I sort of wished he was. I wanted things to be normal. I handed him my trip-sheet and key and told him I was through for the day. He nodded, then told me Hogan wanted to see me. I said thanks and walked into the hall. I knew that Rollo knew everything. His lack of body language told me. His skin and bones were mum. He was being polite. This is what happens when reality invades Rocky Cab. Rollo becomes almost human.

I went upstairs and knocked on Hogan's door. He told me to come in. I won't describe our conversation. I won't even ask you to use your imagination. I told Hogan everything that had happened, and he told me that I wouldn't be charged for my daily lease.

"It'll be credited to your next shift," he said.

Meaning I could drive for free the next time I showed up for work. This struck me as about as ironic as my life ever gets, because this was doubtless the least-profitable day of driving I had ever experienced—not counting my first day fourteen years earlier. But the first day is automatically terrible for every driver. It doesn't even count. I netted five dollars on my first day as a newbie. You never talk about that when you brag about having a really bad day during bull sessions with your fellow hacks. It's considered bad form. After all, anybody can fail on his first day, but it takes a genuine blockhead to eat his lease after fourteen years.

I left the building and crossed the lot to my '64 Chevy. My car had been stolen dozens of times since I had bought it. It's always stolen from the parking lot behind my apartment building, and then recovered by the police who always find it within a mile radius of my crow's nest. The first time it got stolen I was furious, but after awhile I got used to it.

Whenever I walked outside to go to work and saw that my car was missing, I would sigh and walk back inside and call the police and ask them to keep an eye out for it. It got to be embarrassing. The police dispatcher learned my name. I never learned hers. It got to the point where she would chuckle when she heard my voice. But my stolen car was as close as I had ever gotten to authentic criminal activity. This doesn't include the times the police picked me up for murder, kidnapping, etc., because I was always exonerated. By this I mean there never were any murders or kidnappings in the first place. They were just wacky misunderstandings. It gets complicated. Let's move on.

I climbed into my car and looked at my wristwatch. It was four o'clock. I theoretically had three hours left on my lease, and I was down seventy-five bucks for the day. I suddenly had the craving to get back into 123 and see if I could pull out all the stops and earn seventy-five dollars in three hours. It was like a challenge that tempted me only because I knew it wasn't going to happen. "Hold me back, boys," as they say in fake fistfights.

It was at this point that I realized I had not mentioned the stolen five dollars in my witness statement.

I froze, even though I wasn't moving. I guess you could say my mind froze. Then my shoulders drooped. It was just like the times when I was trying to write novels and had completed a chapter and suddenly realized I had forgotten some plot element or scene or bit of dialogue that had inspired me in the first place. I was so busy worrying about crap like style that it got left out.

I started to shake my head with disgust, but I was tired and I was hungry, so I decided instead to buy a hamburger. I could shake my head with disgust after dinner, if I had the strength. And I knew why I was tired. I had been running on a low-voltage infusion of adrenaline ever since the cops had blocked me in. Add to that mix everybody's guns—cops and robber alike—and my nerves were like a wet Fizzie.

I started the engine and drove out of the lot. It felt strange to be heading home at four in the afternoon. My life is pretty rigidly structured for a person who does nothing. Monday, Wednesday, and Friday I work from seven a.m. until seven p.m. That's the structure. The slightest variation tosses me for a loop. When I was a kid our family owned a female sheltie dog. She slept at night in a little doghouse in the backyard. One day my sisters decided the dog was uncomfortable on the wooden floor, so they spent the entire afternoon installing a rug in her house. They had gotten an end-piece from a neighbor who was redoing his living room. That was what made my sisters suddenly think the dog was uncomfortable. They found a scrap of carpet.

The next morning we came outside and found the rug torn to shreds and scattered all over the backyard. The dog had spent the night ripping it out. She was exhausted. She was asleep in the doghouse. My sisters freaked. Their plan, their good deed, their dream of greatness, had been shattered. They ran into the house crying. I walked to the drugstore and ate a chocolate sundae, and waited for the tide to ebb.

Now I was like that sheltie. My Utopian world had been disrupted. Even though I was tired, I felt like I ought to be "doing" something. That shows you how traumatized I was by the events of the afternoon, not to mention the tooth-grinding frustrations of the morning. Frankly, I have always cast a jaundiced eye on people who "do" things, and now there I was, wanting to be just like them. I was forced to conclude that the entire human race lived in a perpetual state of trauma. This caused me to take pity on the people that I used to smirk at. Previously I had thought that people who "did" things were just showing off.

Live and learn.

Of course the thing I felt I ought to be "doing" was driving my cab. The fact that I wasn't doing it meant I would be doing it the next day, Tuesday, my regular break from doing the thing I don't want to do at all, which is work. Not that I mind cab driving. That's much ado about nothing. In fact, driving a cab is to work what absolute zero is to molecular vibrations. In theory it is impossible to arrive at absolute zero where molecules literally cease to move. By the same token, it's impossible to do less than drive a cab, short of doing nothing at all. That's why I took up novel writing in my youth. The way I had it figured, one good bestseller and I would arrive at absolute zero. I envisioned this taking place on a beach in Tahiti. I would show the scientific world a thing or two.

I pulled into a Burger King. As I paid at the drive-up window for my hamburger I started thinking that I could take advantage of this three-hour hiatus by starting a new novel after I got home. I had arrived at a place that I call "the little dream," which is the dream of all novelists to find some free time to write. It's true that I did not work four out of seven days a week, but I was thinking in terms of abnormal free time. It was like winning ten bucks on a scratch ticket, "found money" so to speak, that I could use to buy something I had not been planning on buying. But because I never buy things that I hadn't been planning on buying, this always forced me to think up something to buy, and I had enough trouble thinking up plots for novels without thinking up crap to buy at K-Mart. Ergo, a little bit of money is like a little bit of knowledge—it just gets in my way. I really ought to quit buying scratch tickets.

CHAPTER 9

When I got home I sat at the kitchen table and ate my burger and drank a beer. I didn't turn on the TV. It felt "wrong" to watch TV at this hour on a Monday. I knew that *Gilligan's Island* was being broadcast on cable from a Chicago station. I always catch it at this time of day on Tuesday and Thursday. For some reason, the program director in the windy city changes the afternoon schedule around on Saturday. Why, I don't know. What the hell is so special about Saturday? Is that when the home of the hawk is taken over by nitwits?

I drifted into the living room. I reached into my shirt pocket and pulled out the cash that I had spent the entire day trying to juggle without dropping. To hell with it. I didn't even count it. I just shoved it into *Lolita* and sat down on my easy chair. I knew I was minus seventy-five bucks. That's all I needed to know. But then I remembered that Hogan was giving me a free shift on Tuesday.

All of a sudden the paradigm changed. Holy cow! I was short only five bucks!

I hate money. I had been experiencing a pretty good run of the doldrums there—another five minutes and I would have been singing the blues. But all of a sudden I was lighthearted. I made some quick calculations. On Tuesday morning I would only have to fork over ten dollars for gas and I would be set for the day—and I already had five dollars in profit.

"Hold it," I ordered myself.

I got up and grabbed *Lolita* by the spine and dug out the five-dollar bill that Willie Loman-Sutton had given to me. I walked into the bed-room and slipped it into the New Testament and washed my hands of the whole thing.

I realized that if I tried to figure out where I stood with the extra five dollars in relation to the ten bucks for gas I would have a nervous breakdown, so I decided to just get rid of it and start over at Square One, my favorite geometrical shape. It was like absolute zero, although I wasn't certain that starting over was analogous to absolute zero if you also pos-sessed a desire to earn money the next day—the "desire" part was like a subtle molecular vibration.

I shrugged and went back into the living room and grabbed the re-mote control and headed for Chicago. I arrived just in time to catch the last bar of the closing song from *Gilligan's Island*. The irony made me chuckle. My day had been a study in waves and troughs. Not to worry though. In one hour a Los Angeles station would be carrying me back to the island.

I decided to take advantage of the lull to work on a novel. I had a full hour of free time to think up a plot. I just hoped I could concentrate while knowing that in one hour Mary Ann would be waiting for me with open arms and that spectacular Pepsodent smile.

I turned off the TV and sat down in my easy chair and closed my eyes. This is how I always begin writing a novel. I do absolutely nothing for twenty minutes. It allows me to "let go" of the consternations of the day and make room for the free flow of ideas. It's sort of like Transcen-dental Meditation except that instead of saying a mantra I envision each of my problems as a helium balloon that I release into the air, where they rise into the stratosphere and pop!

After my mind was empty, I started thinking about money. I did this deliberately. It's an integral step in the process of devising plots, since I write for money. It inspires me to greater heights of creativity. I am always suspicious whenever I meet a writer who says he doesn't write for money.

Why would anybody not do something for money? I can't think of a better reason to not do something.

I must have come up short one balloon that evening because dwelling on money made me think about the saucepan of pennies the old lady had tried to foist off on me. It probably weighed a ton. I heard her saying, "You made me lose count!"

Lose count? A doorbell rings and you can't remember mumbling, "two hundred and forty-three"?

But I told myself that this was just a part of her scam. I believed me. Again I wondered how many cab drivers she had pulled that on. And how many would she pull it on in the future?

I started to fume. I started thinking that if she hadn't suckered me, I would have left her house ten minutes earlier than I had, which meant I never would have been sitting outside the Glendale Bank & Trust when an armed robber tapped on my window and secretly held a gun on me at all times. The woman had made me cool my heels on the porch while she pretended she was counting her dusty pennies. Thanks to her petty deceit, my life had been put in jeopardy.

Suddenly I looked forward to going to work on Tuesday morning. The first thing I intended to do was go back to her house and knock on her door and demand my eight bucks. And if she didn't want to give it up, I had a couple of detective acquaintances who just might make her see things differently. Between Willie Sutton and Grandma Moses the city of Denver was getting ripped off. What was this world coming to? By god, when I was a boy, old people were feeble! Suddenly I recalled an episode of *Andy Griffith* where a little old lady sold Barney Fife a used car that turned out to be a lemon. I especially liked the part where the horn slid out of the steering wheel like a snake aimed right at Barney's nose. What a knee-slapper!

By that time I had forgotten all about writing a novel. I got up and paced the living room, thinking about the next day. Never had I felt so motivated to work on a Tuesday. I kept glancing at my wristwatch, wishing the hands would take off like propellers. But isn't that the way of the world? Earlier in the day I had wished I could tie a couple of anvils to the hands of my wristwatch and make the sun slow down, although I did realize that this was a scientific impossibility since there is no proven connection between the movement of watch hands and the rotation of the earth.

The next thing I knew it was time to hit the sack.

When I woke up on Tuesday morning I literally threw the cover off my bed. The blanket knocked over my reading lamp. For a moment I was afraid the ensuing crash might blow a fuse in the building. That's the most embarrassing thing I do in my apartment. I always have to go downstairs and talk to the kid who manages the place and explain what a blanket was doing five feet above my floor.

But everything was copacetic.

I washed up, put on my taxi uniform, loaded my T-shirt with starting cash, made a quick cheese sandwich, grabbed a cold soda, and was out the door at twenty to seven. I ate on the run. I wasn't going to be sitting in front of any hotels that day. I was filled with a form of energy that comes from knowing who you are, what you can do, and how you're going to do it. It was as if I was looking at a map of myself, and right smack in the middle were the words: "You Are Here."

I was centered, baby. I was focused. I was determined to make my nut in record time. For starters I was going straight to the old lady's house, pick up my eight bucks, and spend the rest of the day working The Hill, circling my crow's nest like a vulture circling a corpse. The analogy sort of disintegrated there, but so what? I wasn't driving to please the literary critics. I would leave that up to limousine drivers, the snoots of the literary world.

I walked into the on-call room and got in line behind the other cabbies waiting to pick up their trip-sheets. I heard whispering. I knew what they were saying: "Isn't that the guy who was involved in the bank robbery yesterday? What's he doing here? He ought to be in a sanitarium recovering from shock."

But I understood. I myself couldn't have thought up a better excuse to stay home from work.

An alibi like a robbery comes along once in a lifetime, and you gotta milk it. But I had one small problem. I didn't have anybody to dupe. No wife, no parents, and no brother letting me live with him while I got my act together. When you're a little kid you can fool your mother into thinking you have a cold so you can stay home from school, but my Maw was in Wichita, and remaining prostrate in bed for a week would be pointless if I didn't have someone to bring me chicken soup and heap pity on me. What a wasted bank robbery.

Rollo was all business that morning. Somber. Serious. I could tell it was eating him alive to give me a free lease. I pretended to be all business, too, but he could tell I was laughing on the inside. It was too sweet for words, too easy, and we both knew it, so we saved our ammo to dogfight another day.

I walked out of the on-call room, found my taxi, made a quick check for dents, then climbed in and drove out of the parking lot. Destination: justice.

I would have preferred to skip gassing up until I visited the old lady, which was theoretically possible. The needle on the gas gauge was a hair to the plus side of the red line, so I had five to seven miles worth of gas, but I didn't want to take a chance. I drove to a filling station on Colorado Boulevard that was on a direct route to her house rather than making my usual viaduct detour. I chose one of those mammoth places where the cashier sits in a booth the size of an outhouse. Twenty pumps and no waiting. The downside was the price: two cents more per gallon for unleaded. But I wasn't driving for money that day, I was cruising for revenge. Kenny Rogers said it best: "… don't count your money until the game is done …"

As you might surmise, I had worked myself into what I shall label "a state of mind." In retrospect, I can only conclude that the failures of Monday, combined with the bank robbery and the image of a man with a gun sitting in my backseat, filled me with a desire to make yesterday not be.

It truly had been the worst day of my cab-driving career and I've had some lulus. The key, in my addled mind, to erasing Monday was to go to the address on Capitol Hill where the old lady lived and make her count out eight hundred pennies in my presence, and then let her watch as I sauntered away with the soul of her scam in my pocket.

I pulled out onto Colorado and headed south toward 13th, the street that would take me to the woman's house, the same street that took me to my crow's nest every day, the street that I had kissed on Monday afternoon. I had never before thought about the fact that I lived on a street numbered unlucky by gamblers: Street Thirteen.

My shoulders drooped.

I pulled around a corner and parked in front of the woman's house. I wondered if she owned it. Given her proclivity for not paying cabbies, she could afford it. Six bucks a week times fifty-two weeks times …

I shut it off along with my engine. It's a good thing I'm not good at math or I'd finish all my computations and get really depressed.

I climbed out and walked up the steps and rang the doorbell. She was probably inside counting a yearful of pennies. Eight hundred times fifty-two times …

The knob rattled.

The door opened a few inches. I noticed that there was a chain stretched across the opening.

She peered out at me. "Yes?"

I reached up and pinched the bill of my cap. "Good morning, ma'am."

She didn't nod or speak.

"I'm from the Rocky Mountain Taxicab Company," I said.

Nothing.

"I drove you home from the clinic yesterday morning and you didn't pay me."

"You made me lose count!"

At least she didn't deny it. But this made me think she not only had pulled the scam before but had been accosted by drivers like myself, and thus had her story down pat.

"I'm sorry ma'am, but if you don't pay me, I will have to call the police."

Here's the thing: whenever a cab driver gets cheated by a customer and calls for assistance from the police, the policeman is always on the side of the driver. Next to being a policeman, cab driving is the most dangerous occupation in America. I don't want to belabor this, but when a cab driver is murdered on the job, the cops seem to take it personally. Maybe it's because cops and cabbies work in the same vulnerable place: a car. Their lifeline is a radio, and they work the same AO (area of operations): the streets of Denver, or New York, or LA, Tulsa, Seattle, Houston, Des Moines, but it's all the same street—The Mean Street.

"I owe you nothing!" the woman said. "You walked away!"

She had me there.

Then I thought, suppose I actually called the police, and a cop listened to both our stories, especially the part where I had walked away after saying, "Keep your pennies."

Would he cast a jaundiced eye at me?

It was like a wake-up call. Suddenly I wondered what the hell I was doing badgering an old lady over eight bucks. As I have said many times before: I need some kind of goddamn therapy.

She slammed the door shut.

I needed that.

I needed it bad.

Real bad.

I turned and walked on eggs down to my taxi. I climbed in and sat there trying to make sense out of the last twenty-four hours, especially the part where I had devised a plan of revenge against a woman old enough to have played hopscotch in grade school with Bernadette Clancy.

Bernadette Clancy is my mother's maiden name.

I decided there was only one thing to do: turn off my brain. With any luck, that would prevent me from going back to my crow's nest, calling Wichita, and apologizing to my Maw. I stopped making strange phone calls to Maw when I lived in Cleveland. She insisted on it.

CHAPTER 10

I was sitting in front of the Brown Palace Hotel eating a Twinkie and sipping a cup of 7-11 joe. There were four cabs in front of me. My Rocky radio was turned off, and I had a paperback in my left hand. You might have thought it was a typical taxi Wednesday, but it was still Tuesday.

I had driven away from the penny lady twenty minutes earlier, stopped at a 7-11 on Colfax, then headed for the hotels in midtown. I wasn't choosy. The cabstand at the Brown Palace was as good a stand as any, and better than most. The way I had it figured, I was never going to get any therapy, so I might as well pretend in a good way. I decided I would just do things the way I had always done them, which might have the effect of erasing Monday from my mind forever. What did I know about psychotherapy? I was winging it.

I had already wasted half an hour on The Hill but it didn't really matter because if I had originally driven to the Brown after gassing up I would probably be fourth in line instead of fifth. Sometimes you pull up at a stand and you're the only cab there, and a customer comes out and you go right to DIA. Sometimes you sit for an hour before you get a fare. Every day is different even though every day is the same: a hotel, a bell, a Twinkie, and a joe. Then on April 15th you send Sam the same ol' cut and continue to dream The Big Dream. That has to do with selling a novel, but let's move on.

In my experience, the main drawback to cab driving is getting ensnared in what I call The Positioning Game. You start thinking that if I had done this I would now be first in line instead of fifth. Or if I had done that I would be driving a fare to DIA instead of Safeway. You become as crazed as a sourdough running all over the desert looking for the mother lode. But in cab driving there is no mother lode. Oh sure, once in awhile you get a fare to Vail or Aspen, but so what? You can't retire on the windfall. Ergo, it's best not to think about what might have happened if you had done this instead of that. You have to take the long view of things. Which is to say, if you had gotten a degree in computer programming instead of English you might be earning eighty grand a year right now instead of driving a taxi. Now that's something to think about.

"One twenty-three."

I picked up the mike. "One twenty-three."

"Go to channel four."

I reached to the squawk box and switched from Channel 1 to Channel 4.

"One twenty-three," I said.

"Murph," the Channel 4 dispatcher said, "Hogan wants you to call him at his office. Are you near a phone?"

"Check."

He's waiting."

"Check."

Well, at least it wasn't an L-2. I didn't know what the record was, but I suspected I had been given more L-2's than any driver in the history of Rocky Cab. L-2 means you have to return to the motor, usually to talk to Hogan about something that neither of you wants to talk about. Sometimes a violation of taxi rules, sometimes a murder. You never know, so it's unpleasant to answer an L-2. As you might surmise from what I just said, they don't tell you ahead of time what's up, they just tell you to come in right away. It's similar to an order in the army given by an officer. Similar, hell—it's exactly the same.

I hung up my mike and got out of 123 and walked back to the taxi parked behind me. It was a Yellow Cab. I had to tell the driver that I would be off-duty for the next five minutes and that he should drive around my taxi if the line moved forward. It was a courtesy thing.

I hate courtesy. It causes me to talk to people I would rather not talk to for a variety of reasons. This goes back a ways, but I had once been a critical factor in what I can only describe as a "nationwide wager" that caused countless Yellow drivers to lose rather large sums of money. Don't ask me to explain it. I barely understand it myself, except the part where I had absolutely nothing to do with it. That's how I end up in the middle of most messes. They grow around me in the way a pearl grows around a pebble.

I didn't recognize the Yellow driver, thank God. He may have been a newbie. For some reason the turnover rate of drivers at Yellow isn't as high as at Rocky. I might as well be honest here. When Rocky drivers get really good at taxi driving, they move up to Yellow Cab and work for them. I will have to say that in the pecking order of Denver cab companies, Rocky sits at the bottom of the barrel, or the ladder, or whatever dismal metaphor you prefer. Our vehicles are rather old. More than once I have heard the word "rickety" bandied about the on-call room. On the plus side, Rocky has the lowest lease-rate of any cab company in town. Need I say more? Yes. Another advantage of remaining at Rocky forever is that you become a kind of demigod to the newbies. Sure, a Rocky demigod is the equivalent of a mediocre Yellow driver, but as I've often stated, when you drive a taxi for a living you don't get that many opportunities to feel "special." And anyway, I think of the Rocky Mountain Taxicab Company as the Minor Leagues where the John Elways and Lawrence Oliviers of tomorrow make their bones. I mixed a few metaphors there, so that'll give you something to unravel while I call Hogan.

I walked into the Brown Palace and went downstairs to the hallway that leads to the magnificent men's room. The men's room at the Brown is made of brown marble. When you use the can at the Brown you feel like the head honcho in the Valley of the Kings. They also have a pay phone down there. I dropped a quarter in and dialed Hogan's number. I memorized it long, long ago.

"Yeah," Hogan said into the receiver, as if he was unenthusiastically acknowledging an uninteresting fact in the hopes that the conversation would wither.

"Murph here, boss."

"Oh Murph, great, thanks for calling back so soon."

I have never understood why Hogan brightens up when he talks to me. End of observation.

"Detectives Ottman and Quigg got in touch with me ten minutes ago," he said. "From what I understand, they caught the bank robbery suspect."

I closed my eyes and sighed right there by the men's room door. I didn't give a damn who was watching, which I normally do. I keep a tight leash on my emotions in the vicinity of public restrooms.

"That's good to hear," I said.

"But here's the deal, Murph. They have him in custody at Denver General Hospital and they want to know if you can get over there right away."

"Sweet Jaysus ... did they shoot him?"

"I don't know. But they want you there as fast as possible. They didn't give me any details. You know detectives."

Oh yeah.

I know detectives.

I know four.

We rang off. I was barely halfway up the staircase to the main floor when I felt adrenaline leaking into my spine. I was ambivalent about this. In some ways adrenaline can be fun, especially if you're watching a monster movie. As a matter of social propriety though, I try to avoid adrenaline before noon, so twice in one morning was just plain gauche.

I walked out of the hotel.

And froze.

There were no cabs at the stand, except mine. Four people were waiting at the curb with suitcases, and they were looking right at me. William, a black doorman who has served as a palace guard at the Brown longer than I have been driving a taxi, hurried toward me with an eager expression.

"You got yourself a good trip here, my man," he said in a muted tone of voice. "Two separate couples going to the airport, and they're both willing to pay full fair."

I nearly had a heart attack. He was talking one hundred dollars. This was virtually unheard of. I am not exaggerating when I say this was the stuff of legend.

"I hate to tell you this, William, but I can't take them."

"What!"

"I'm off duty. The police want to talk to me. I have to go see them right away."

He pulled his head back and parted his lips, but didn't say anything. We stared at each other. It was as if my Univac and his Univac had linked up telepathically and we were trading data at the speed of light, analyzing the situation, evaluating the facts, and projecting the results, rendering our vocal chords useless.

"Lord," he finally whispered.

Then a Yellow Cab drifted around the corner and casually, obliviously, pulled up behind my taxi.

William shook his head and hurried over to speak to the Yellow driver.

I walked desultorily to my cab and climbed in. I started the engine, then waited until the Yellow driver had pulled his cab around mine to the canopy that overhangs the front door of the Brown. I drove away from the curb.

"Don't look back," a voice said. It wasn't mine. I don't know who said it. I was too stricken to care.

I made my way over to Broadway and headed south to 8th Avenue. That's where DGH is located. That's where the bank robber was in custody—the man who had stolen an undetermined amount of money from the Glendale Bank & Trust and one hundred dollars in DIA money from me.

I turned in at the hospital entry and made my way around the U-shaped drive, looking for a parking space in the big lot that fronts the building. No dice. I drove across the street to the next closest lot and found a slot. I had to pay a dollar. Normally cab drivers hate to use commercial parking lots, but I was in no mood to uphold tradition. I rarely am.

I crossed over and entered the hospital. Like all people, I hate hospitals, so I wasn't looking forward to the rigmarole of dealing with the clerk at the information desk. So imagine my thrill when I saw Detective Quigg standing by the desk. He was waiting for me. He escorted me to an elevator. I felt "special."

"The man is in the cardiac unit," Quigg informed me as we rode upstairs. "He's unconscious. We need you to I.D. him."

I nodded. I had a million questions, but knew not to ask any of them. I played it cool. I needed the practice.

We stepped into a waiting room. He led me to the end of a hallway where a uniformed policeman was seated on a folding chair. It was like TV. That made everything seem real.

Quigg stopped and turned to me. "Let me explain what's going on here," he said in a muted tone of voice. He sounded just like William. My shoulders drooped. "This man was found unconscious yesterday afternoon lying in a parking lot about a mile away from the Glendale Bank & Trust. He was brought to the hospital by ambulance. Right now I would like you to step into the room, take a good look at him, and let me know whether or not you think it's the man that was in your cab yesterday, the same man you encountered at the bank."

I nodded. This obligation made me feel "important" but not very "special." I'll take special any day over important. When you do important things, there's an implication that people are relying on you.

I walked into the hospital room and saw the man on a bed. His upper body was covered by a plastic tent. A nurse was standing by. She pulled the plastic aside. I looked at the patient. He had wires connected to his body. I'm not ashamed to say that it made my skin crawl. This was Full-Blown Reality. Need I say more?

It was definitely the robber—although he bore no actual resemblance to Dustin Hoffman. He appeared to be in his mid-sixties, was white-haired, and had a sort of elongated face. Well, maybe he did look a little like Dustin Hoffman.

I turned and walked back out to the hall.

"It's him," I said.

"You're sure now?" Quigg said.

I nodded.

"Do you want to take a second look?" Quigg said. "I want you to be absolutely certain, Mr. Murphy. I know it's hard to do this. I know it's difficult to remember someone's face when you weren't expecting to have to identify him to the police, especially when his physical condition is different than the first time you saw him. This is very important."

I swallowed hard. "I'm sure it's him," I said. Then I said, "Is he going to die?" On my question list, that was #1 out of one million.

"The doctors say he's in bad shape," Quigg said. He shrugged.

I wanted to ask question #2: "Did the bank get their money back?" And question #3: "Did you find the gun?" But I didn't ask any of them. Reality renders moot all things irrelevant, just as death renders moot all things relevant. Life is a mayfly.

But—"Did the bank get their money back?" I suddenly said, trying to trivialize things back to normal.

Quigg looked me in the eye. "I'm sorry, Mr. Murphy, but I can't discuss that aspect of the case."

I nodded. I hated myself for asking that, but I knew why I had done it. I wanted to be in-with-the-in-crowd. That's one of the seven warning signs of humanity. Cops always make me feel human. It's not a good feeling.

Quigg thanked me for taking time off from work to come in and make the identification. He said he would be in touch with me again—but that was only because I was a crucial witness in a bank robbery and not a member of the in-crowd.

When I walked out of the hospital I felt neither important nor special. I felt lousy.

CHAPTER 11

I got back into my taxi and drove out of the DGH lot. I turned on my Rocky radio. I was going to try to make a habit out of using the radio from now on. It felt unnatural. It reminded me of the time I tried to make a habit out of smoking cigarettes. I choked and coughed but eventually was able to take a long drag off a cig without collapsing. But isn't that always the first step in revamping your life? You're doing something you've never done before, and it feels unnatural. Beginners always look and feel foolish, whether smoking or driving or dancing or—well— I guess I should throw in sex. I'm sure some of us are adults here.

But the reason I took up smoking when I was seventeen was because I wasn't cool. I was a senior in high school, and it seemed like everywhere I looked I saw cool people, and they all smoked. Humphrey Bogart smoked. James Bond smoked. John Lennon smoked.

Of course they also had jobs, but I concentrated on the smoking part.

It was a struggle. I practiced smoking when I was alone in my bedroom. Both of my parents smoked cigars in those days, so I didn't have the problem that beleaguers most beginners. Cigar smoke trumps cigarette smoke any day. I could puff away in my bedroom without my Maw pounding on the door and asking if I was burning my mattress again. That's another story that I don't want to get into, except to say that it involved a chemistry set and a misunderstanding of the definition of the word "milligram."

But I figured that if I took up smoking, all the kids in school would think I was cool. They would invite me to parties and ask for my opinion on Carnaby Street fashions and the art of Peter Max. But by the time I reached the point where I could smoke without coughing, high school ended. So there I was with a useless habit and nobody to impress.

Anyway, the problem with listening to the Rocky radio was that I couldn't listen to the AM radio at the same time. The cacophony would have been unendurable, especially during guitar solos. I have never gotten over the fact that every disk jockey in America feels compelled to talk during the opening bars of rock 'n' roll records, such as "Fun, Fun, Fun," by the Beach Boys. The opening bars are often a big highlight of a song, and there's some motormouth DJ talking over the intro and stopping at the very exact moment that the rockers start singing "... hereonradiostation KZOD Well she got her daddy's car ..." and thus ruining my life.

Aah, why complain? It's all a racket.

I drove desultorily back toward the Brown Palace and listened to the dispatcher offering bells. I looked at my wristwatch. It was a little after nine a.m. I had gone two hours without making any money. I ought have grossed at least twenty two dollars by then. Every driver has his own formula that he tries to adhere to in order to earn maximum profits for the day. For some drivers it's twenty dollars an hour average with a seventeen-dollar minimum. It differs. In order to make my fifty-dollar profit per day I have to gross $130.00. I shoot for eleven dollars an hour, which gives me $132.00. If I earn ten dollars and eighty cents an hour for twelve hours I make $129.60, which leaves me forty cents short. I probably don't have to explain to you what that does to my mind. So I just earn eleven dollars an hour and try not to let the extra two-dollar profit at the end of the day throw me for a loop.

I knew I had to start jumping bells. I was playing catch-up again. This was rare because troughs are almost always followed by waves. In scientific circles, two troughs without an intervening wave wouldn't be just an anomaly, it would be literally impossible. But cab driving is not a science, it is an art, and you can get away with all sorts of impossibilities in art. Look at Jackson Pollock.

I decided to avoid hotels because I knew for a fact that I could make at least twenty dollars an hour by taking calls off the radio. But "knowing" isn't "doing." By this I mean that having a theory down pat isn't the same thing as applying the theory. This ought to lead me to the subject of writing novels, but it won't. Ironically, when it comes to writing novels, I spend more time doing than knowing, but let's move on.

I hung a right at 14th Avenue and drove past the Capitol building with its inspirational golden dome glinting in the springtime sunlight. Back when I first arrived in Denver I tried to find an apartment with a view of the dome. I felt it would inspire me to keep trying to write commercial novels—but again, let's move on.

"Capitol Hill."

I grabbed the mike. When a cabbie makes a commitment to work the radio, he always keeps the microphone in his right hand, but since I've always had issues with commitment I had forgotten that crucial part of earning money, so I didn't have the mike ready. But luck was with me.

"One twenty-three."

"Botanic Gardens."

"Check."

The Botanic Gardens is an interesting place. The name pretty much describes it. It's sort of a museum for things that grow, like flowers. It's a jungle in the middle of the city. It covers a couple acres up near 10th and York. I once got dragged there by a girlfriend on an afternoon date. I have nothing against flowers, but you have to really be into standing around in order to enjoy the place. We spent two hours standing around looking at floral exhibits. Then she wanted to go to the Museum of Natural History over at City Park. That was last time I ever dated in the afternoon.

I turned south on York and drove up the hill to the entrance to the Gardens. There's a wide space there at the curb for a bus stop, so I pulled in.

Beyond the BG gate is a massive structure like a long geodesic dome. It rises majestically out of the foliage. It reminds me of the domed buildings in *The Time Machine*. I like looking at it whenever I drive by because it makes me think of The Future. Not mine, just the future in general.

I shut off the engine and hoped I wouldn't have to go to the entrance and ask a ticket clerk who had called a cab. That's the drawback to answering bells in public arenas. They can be as bad as phone booths in terms of no-shows. But I didn't have to get out and go to the entrance. I saw them coming at me. Two ladies. Old ladies. They were wearing print dresses and carrying purses. They were also wearing hats. The whole shooting match.

I had to get out of my cab after all. I hopped out and hurried around to the right-rear door and held it open for them.

"Are you the driver we called for?" one of them said.

"Yes, ma'am," I replied. I was now.

I waited while they took forever to get in. But they were more sprightly than the two Hobbits whom I had picked up at the Havana Bank. These ladies managed to shave ten seconds off forever.

I hurried around to the driver's side and hopped in. I was trying to fight off a bad feeling that kept trying to get its hooks into me. This had not been a good week for old ladies and me, but I didn't want to develop a psychological tic. I once delivered flowers for a living and I accidentally walked in on a corpse at a mortuary. It gave me a psychological tic.

"Where are you ladies going?" I said.

"Well, we can't decide whether we want to have lunch at Biloxi's Restaurant or go shopping at Cherry Creek first," one of them said.

Biloxi's is a ritzy slop-joint at Cherry Creek North, which is across the street from the shopping center. It was six to one and a half-dozen to the other, since I wasn't going to make more money either way. Note that I did not say, "six of one and half-dozen of the other." That's what everybody says. A long time ago I decided that of all the idioms that people screw up, I would allow this to be the only one that irritated me. After all, given the numerous rejection slips I've received, who am I to play English professor?

"If you would like my opinion, you should dine first," I said, trying to move things along. "That way you'll have lots of energy for shopping."

"That sounds like a good idea," the other lady said. "Why don't we do that?" It was like a conference between Eisenhower and Patton.

I dropped my flag and turned on the meter. Look out Rommel.

Cherry Creek was three dollars away. But that included the automatic dollar-fifty flag-drop, plus any tip. They ended up giving me five bucks. That's how you do it.

I smiled to myself. I almost felt normal. I pulled back onto 1st Avenue to drive by the Cherry Creek cabstand and see if it was vacant. The odds were against it, and the odds were right. Three cabs. I wasn't going to sit at the stand for an hour waiting for a rich lady to come out of Saks. But you have to make the run past the stand if you are serious about earning money. If you can position yourself first in line at Cherry Creek, it's a good place to listen to the radio, since Cherry Creek is so close to so many main arteries—Colorado Boulevard, University Boulevard, First Avenue. You can get anywhere fast, and you might even luck into a Saks fare. But if there is even one taxi at the stand, I keep driving. "He who lives by the mall, dies by the mall."

I headed west on 1st Avenue, which turned into Speer Boulevard. I was thinking about working my way back up to Capitol Hill when I got an L-2.

"One twenty-three, el-two."

I picked up the mike.

"Check."

I hung up the mike.

L-2.

I knew what that meant. Either the bank robber had died, or

something else had happened. Well ... I guess I didn't know what it meant except in abstract terms, or at least in psychological terms. Which is to say, I felt lousy again. Whatever it was, it would be bad news. Hogan never gave me an L-2 to tell me I won the lottery.

I turned my cab around and headed back toward Cherry Creek to take University north to the motor. If I had gotten the L-2 when I was at Cherry Creek I could have headed right up University. I was playing The Positioning Game again. If only this had happened instead of that.

The thing about The Positioning Game is that it's played more often by drivers who are serious about making money than by drivers who sit in front of hotels, i.e., it's played by crazed sourdoughs. So I was a bit irritated by the fact that I had been interrupted before I had gotten really crazed—I had been sort of looking forward to it. But I "went with the flow." I knew that after this business with the bank robber was resolved, I would have the rest of my life to work hard. That really took the wind out of my sails.

I pulled into the parking lot at the motor and got out, leaving my briefcase and toolbox and a Twinkie on the front seat. I walked into the on-call room and didn't even look at Rollo. I walked past the cage and entered the hallway and climbed the stairs to Hogan's office.

I knocked on the door.

"Come in," Hogan said.

This indicated to me that Ottman and Quigg were with him. Hogan normally says "Yeah," in the same tone of voice that a juvenile delinquent says "Yuh" when a high-school counselor asks if he's going to buckle down and study harder.

I pushed the door open. Ottman and Quigg were standing by his desk. No surprise. They were standing where Duncan and Argyle used to stand whenever I was called in on suspicion of murder. Ergo, I just walked over and sat down on "my" chair as I had come to think of it.

"Nice you see you again, gentlemen," I said in a casual though not flippant manner. I was trying to come off as forthright, like an admiral in a movie about Pearl Harbor who had been given "the bad news" and had called a meeting of his staff. No point in dwelling on what might have been. We have business that needs attending to. All right, Ensign Quigg, where's the U.S.S. *Normandy* cruising at this moment?

"Two hundred miles east of Wake Island, sir."

"Thanks for coming in."

"No problem, Detective Quigg," I said. "How can I help you?"

Quigg glanced at Ottman.

"We need to ask you some questions, Mr. Murphy," Ottman said.

"Please … call me Murph. To be perfectly frank, gentlemen, I have never liked being called Mister Murphy. I associate the phonics too closely with such fictional characters as Mister Greenjeans, Mister Jingle-Dingle, and Mister Moose."

Ottman glanced at Quigg, then looked at me. "All right … Murph." Ottman reached toward Hogan's desk, picked up a blank trip-sheet, and held it up for me to see.

"Do you recognize this?"

Correction: it was not totally blank. It had my name and taxi number on it. "It's mine," I said.

"This trip-sheet is dated yesterday," he said.

"That's correct," I said. "That's my Monday trip-sheet."

"None of the boxes are filled in," he said.

"I know," I replied.

There was a moment of silence. Then Ottman said. "Why didn't you fill in the boxes? PUC regulations require that the boxes be filled in."

I rolled my eyes. By this I mean I rotated my eyeballs vertically until my pupils were gazing with disgust at the ceiling. But that takes too long to say and is somewhat awkward. I prefer to just say "rolled my eyes." If some people think this means I literally plucked my eyeballs from my skull and fired them across the floor like marbles, that's their problem.

I'm not here to teach remedial colloquialism to people obsessed with the fraud of naturalistic prose.

"I didn't get around to filling out the trip-sheet prior to the bank robbery," I said.

"Why not?" Ottman said.

That was an interesting question. I thought I had answered it, but on second thought, I could see his point. I had merely "introduced" the answer.

"Well, I was having what we cab drivers refer to as a 'bad day.' On a couple of calls I didn't make any money at all. They were sort of like no-shows. Then I was so busy trying to grab some calls to make up for my losses that I didn't fill out the trip-sheet."

"But why not?"

Again, I thought I had answered that question. This was getting irksome. I felt like I was talking to either a brilliant courtroom lawyer or an idiot.

"I didn't have time," I said.

"How much time would it have taken you to fill out the sheet?" he said.

"A minute," I replied.

"You didn't have an extra minute?"

"Yes."

"You did have an extra minute?"

"Yes."

"Well, then why didn't you fill out the sheet?"

"By extra minute I am referring to real time," I said slowly, as if I was speaking to a courtroom filled with gum-chewing reporters who were hanging on my every word. "When I said I didn't have time, I was speaking metaphorically."

"I don't understand," Ottman said.

Obviously.

I cleared my throat.

"When I am beleaguered by time, or work, or anything else that annoys me, I feel that the rules no longer apply to me. Consequently, I don't always fill out the trip-sheet right after I drop off a customer. I wait until I have a cluster of trips, then I fill them in all at once. It takes a minute."

"So you did have a real minute, but you did not have a metaphorical minute."

"That's correct."

"You do realize don't you, Murph, that the law does not recognize specious reasoning?"

"I have been made somewhat aware of that fact in my time."

"But you went ahead and disobeyed the law anyway?"

"Well ... I wouldn't put it that way. But I mean, yes ... I disobeyed the law. But I wouldn't put it that way."

"What way would you put it, Murph?"

"I would just say that I'm lazy."

He set the trip-sheet back on the desk.

"Since your trip-sheet isn't filled out, would you mind telling us about the fares you picked up yesterday?" Ottman said.

"I don't mind at all," I said. "But can I ask you one question?"

"Go ahead."

"What does this have to do with the bank robbery?"

"It doesn't have anything to do with the bank robbery, Murph."

"It doesn't?"

"No."

"Then why are you here?"

"We're here to investigate an assault complaint."

"Who got assaulted?"

"The complaint was filed by a Mrs. Elsie Jacobs."

The penny lady!

But that wasn't the best part.

"She's at Denver General Hospital right now," Ottman said. "She's in the cardiac care unit. She was brought to the hospital by ambulance this morning after suffering a heart attack."

CHAPTER 12

Suddenly Admiral Brendan Aloysius Murphy of the Sixth Fleet lost all of my aplomb and let my jaw hang wide open. I leaned back against the chair and stared at Detective Ottman. This wasn't merely switching horses in midstream, this was like jumping from a moving train to another train that was highballing in the opposite direction.

Ottman pulled up a folding chair and sat down facing me. Not directly, but at a forty-five degree angle. He was sort of beside me and sort of in front of me. I had the feeling that the next few minutes would determine our physical relationship in a metaphorical as well as a real sense.

He reached to the desk and gently drew the blank trip-sheet toward us. He tapped on the first empty box. "I wonder if you could just walk me through the fares of yesterday," he said.

Detective Quigg reached into his coat pocket and pulled out a small notebook. He reached into his shirt pocket and pulled out a ballpoint pen. He flipped the notebook open and touched the pen to the paper. But he didn't write anything. Oh no. Not then. He waited until I started talking. Then he started writing. The pen made a sound like this: "skritch skritch."

"Please begin with your first fare of the morning," Quigg said.

Right off the bat I did something wrong. I reached up and placed the palms of my hands flat against my face and dragged them down to my chin. I did this to help me think, but suddenly I realized it might have made me look like someone who was slapping his face with remorse after having been "found out." You often see this in bad melodramas. Not that I equate my life with a bad melodrama, but I could.

The reason I did it though was because I had made a vow to myself that I would just forget about yesterday and get on with my life. This is how I always deal with yesterdays, even the good ones. I would say that it works 93 percent of the time. But some yesterdays just can't be forgotten. Apparently the police weren't going to let me forget this one.

"The first fare I picked up was a pedestrian. He flagged me down on the street just after I gassed up at a Seven-Eleven store. But he only wanted to go a couple blocks."

"Do you normally pick up fares off the street?"

"I never do anything normally. I'm flexible in my choice of fares. Maybe a bit too flexible. My decisions are made intuitively."

"How do you mean?"

"Well, I mean whether or not I pick up a pedestrian depends on various factors, such as the time of day, the physical appearance of the flagger, or whether I'm broke. I guess the broke factor is the most common."

"Aren't you always broke when you pick up your first fare of the day?"

"No. Sometimes I just don't have any money."

"Isn't that the same thing as being broke?"

"No."

"What's the difference?"

"Broke is a state of being that occurs only after six o'clock at night. It has to do with the probability factor of picking up a final fare. If I don't have any money after six o'clock at night, I'm broke."

"What about six o'clock in the morning?"

"I never work that early."

"When do you start?"

"Seven."

"All right. What about not having any money after seven in the morning?"

"That's normal. That's not broke."

He stopped asking questions for a moment. I stared at the blank trip-sheet and listened to the steady skritch of Quigg's ballpoint pen. It was a Bic.

"How much money did the fare give you?"

"Three dollars."

Ottman turned to Hogan, who was sitting behind his desk silently staring at me. He always did this when detectives ran me through the meat grinder.

"Mr. Hogan, would it be possible for me to obtain a blank trip-sheet. I would like to fill one out while Murph describes his day. In this way we can see what his trip-sheet would have looked like if he had obeyed PUC regulations."

"Certainly," Hogan said, getting up and going to a filing cabinet.

I didn't look at Hogan. I stared at the nearest wall. The remark about me not obeying regulations gave me an inkling as to where this situation was headed. I call it "the unemployment office."

"Thank you, Mr. Hogan," Ottman said, setting the blank trip-sheet on the desk and pulling out his own Bic. Bic's are well made yet inexpensive. Detectives have to pay for their own Bics. I learned this the hard way.

Ottman asked me exactly where I had picked up the first fare. I gave him the nearest intersection, the time of the pick-up, the time of the drop-off, and the price on the meter. He wrote it down. For all practical purposes, Detective Ottman was now a trained taxi driver.

"Who was your next fare?" Ottman said.

I swallowed hard.

I told him about the penny lady, starting with the brief conversation with the dispatcher about my ability to change a one-hundred-dollar bill, and continuing on to the moment when I walked away without accepting a single coin of the eight hundred pennies. I waited for Ottman to start asking more detailed questions about the woman who was currently lying in the DGH cardiac unit, but he simply filled out the trip-sheet and then looked at me and said, "What was your third fare of the day?"

I swallowed, but not too hard. I felt as if I had "gotten away" with something.

I told him about the kid going to The Ram for a high school reunion pre-luncheon.

Then I told him about the sales lady whom I took to Dagwell's. He did interrupt my narrative to ask if I knew for certain whether she was a sales lady. "Could she have been a customer?" he said.

"Yes," I said.

He didn't ask what made me think she was a sales lady. I was glad, because I had no answer, and I did not want to get into a detailed and possibly embarrassing discussion about the groundless suppositions upon which I base all my assumptions.

"And your next fare?" he said.

"I picked up two ladies at the Havana Bank that is cattycorner from Buckingham Square. This took about a minute, and I made one dollar and seventy cents."

I heard a strange noise come from Hogan's desk. I glanced over at him. He had laughed. I had never heard Hogan laugh before. It was hideous. Yet I understood. He rubbed his mouth as if trying to erase his laugh. I used to do that in grade school. I had a 97 percent success rate. Hogan failed.

By now the trip-sheet was starting to look like the real thing. Ottman wanted me to be very precise about the times I had picked up the fares and dropped them off. It was a bit difficult to remember, but I felt that I was getting the times to within fifteen minutes, which is actually not very good in terms of taxi facts, especially when you are talking to the police, the DA, the prosecutor, the jury, or your cellmate.

I did have one thing going for me though. Throughout my worst day ever I had kept glancing at my wristwatch, and I was able to picture the hands of yesterday. When you're having a bad day, details relevant to the badness often stick with you. They frequently emerge when you are seated on a barstool at Sweeney's telling your troubles to your friends, although in my case it's usually strangers. But isn't this the essence of storytelling anyway? Misery? The how-to books refer to it as "conflict"—but it's simply misery. If a novel doesn't have misery in it, the author is just having fun at the typewriter. Okay. I'll admit it. I've never had any fun at the typewriter. But that hasn't gotten me an acceptance slip.

"And your next fare?" Ottman said.

I took a deep breath. "Well, this was where things started to really fall apart."

"Is this when you picked up the man who is suspected of robbing the bank?'

"Oh no. I would have to say that the 'falling apart' was completed by then. This earlier call came from Arapahoe Road and Chambers Road."

Quigg whistled. It was one of those whistles like a reporter in a 1930s movie would make when he heard astonishing news. It wasn't a wolf whistle, although it held a sonic resemblance. Quigg sort of looked like a reporter with his notebook and whistle. I smiled at him. He might have thought I was smiling at his whistle, but I smiled because he looked like a young Adolfe Menjou. If you don't know who Adolphe Menjou was, it really doesn't matter. Menjou was in *The Front Page* (1937). It was a movie about reporters, although he was an editor.

"The dispatcher had been offering the call for about half an hour, but no taxi drivers had accepted it. I first heard it when I was on Capitol Hill. By the time I worked my way over to Aurora, the call was still open, so I decided to answer it."

"Why did you take so long to decide?"

"Well … you have to understand … it takes me forever to make decisions. But I had earned only fourteen dollars and ninety cents in cash after working four hours …"

The hideous noise came from Hogan's desk again. I glanced over at him and frowned. He yanked out a handkerchief and pretended he had coughed. A feeble ruse, but one that I nevertheless filed away. It had the potential for refinement.

"So I was well on my way to being broke," I continued. "That's what motivated me to jump the bell. It was a trip to DIA, so it looked like all of my financial problems were going to be taken care of in one fell swoop."

"What's that?"

"One fell swoop."

"What's a 'fell swoop'?" Ottman said. "Is that taxi jargon?"

"Why … no … I don't actually … I suppose it could be Shakespearian."

"But what does it mean?" he said.

"Excuse me, Ottman," Quigg said, lifting his pen. "I've heard of 'fell swoop' before. It's like a hawk attacking a rabbit … right?" He looked at me for confirmation.

"That's correct," I said, although I hadn't thought of that. In fact, I had never thought about "fell swoop" at all. I just said it a lot.

I continued to elaborate for Ottman:

"In terms of human beings though, 'fell swoop' is sort of like Michael Corleone wiping out all his enemies with one well-planned, well-timed, and well-engineered mob hit at the end of the first *Godfather*. I decided to take the call because it would make me the equivalent of a smart mobster."

I grinned.

Ottman glanced at his partner, then looked at me.

"Did it work?"

"No."

"What happened?"

"My plan wasn't very well-timed."

"How so?"

"I was too far away to get there on time."

"I believe it," Quigg said as he scribbled.

"It was one of those things that occasionally happen to taxi drivers," I said. "It usually happens only to beginners. I call them 'newbies.' But every once in a great while it happens to old pros, and to me."

"Were the customers gone by the time you arrived?"

"No. The house was in a cul-de-sac, and when I drove in they were loading their luggage into a four-wheel-drive vehicle. When I pulled up, a lady told me that they couldn't wait any longer so they had asked a neighbor to drive them to the airport."

"Even though you were already there?"

"Yes."

"How did you react to the situation?"

"What do you mean?"

"Did you get angry?"

"I never get angry at customers."

"Why not?"

"There's no point. That would be like getting angry at a wave."

"How's that?"

"Customers are like waves."

"What kind of waves?"

"Water waves. Like on an ocean."

"What do you mean by that, Murph?"

"I mean there's always another wave coming along. They just keep coming and coming and coming, and they're all the same, except sometimes you find a big score on one of the waves, but not often enough that you can expect a lot of money from every wave. You mostly find flotsam and jetsam."

"What's jetsam?"

"It's navy lingo."

"So they told you that they already had a ride?"

"Yes."

"And what did you do?"

"I drove around in a circle."

"In anger?"

"No, in the cul-de-sac. In fact, I made only a half-circle. Then I drove away."

"And you didn't argue or make any attempt to change their minds?"

"No."

"That must have set you back in terms of time and money."

"You better believe it."

"How did you feel after you drove away?"

"Well ... I felt resigned to fate. Cab drivers do that a lot."

"But you weren't angry?"

"No."

"Even though you were broke."

"Yes. No. I wasn't angry about being broke. In a sense, I am always broke, so I'm used to it. I suppose if I was a millionaire and didn't have any money, I would be angry."

Ottman glanced at Quigg, then looked at me and raised his chin. "I'm just trying to understand something here, Murph. I hope you don't mind my dwelling on this."

"No. I'm used to the police dwelling on my activities."

"You are?"

"Yes."

"Have the police ever dwelled on your activities before?"

"Yes."

"What police?"

"Duuu ..." I said, then stopped.

I almost said "Duncan and Argyle." Thank goodness I caught myself. It might have sounded flippant. I cleared my throat.

"Detective Duncan and Detective Argyle of the Bureau of Missing Persons down at DPD have run me through the meat ... have interrogated me in the past."

"We know Dunk and Argy," Ottman said with a smile. "What did they interrogate you about?"

"Oh … just some cases they were working on awhile back."

"What cases?"

"Oh … you know … a couple of murders, a kidnapping, a robbery. Just average stuff."

"Were you a suspect?"

I smiled and shrugged my shoulders. "To tell you the truth, Detectives Duncan and Argyle never really made that clear to me. I'm not a mind-reader, you know, but I think they were sort of wondering if I knew something."

"Did you?"

"Yes."

"What did you know?"

"I knew I was innocent. But beyond that I didn't think I was much help to them. They can probably fill you in. They took notes, too."

"All right. Let's get back to the fare on Arapahoe and Chambers. It must have taken you a long time to get down to the address, and just as long to get back to town. On top of that, you made no money at all, correct?"

"Correct."

"So it seems to me that you might have been upset."

"Well … maybe a little."

"Or maybe a lot?" Ottman said.

"No. Just a little. I'm always a little upset."

"About what?"

"Life in general."

"But didn't missing out on a lucrative fare to DIA and wasting so much time make you more upset?"

"No. Nothing makes me more upset than life in general."

Ottman then asked me what time I had gotten the Arapahoe call, what time I had arrived at the address, and the exact time of my next call.

"My next call came at one-thirty."

Ottman looked down at the trip-sheet.

"You dropped off the two women from the Havana Bank at eleven-thirty, and you picked up your next fare at one-thirty?"

"That's correct."

"That's two hours between calls."

"You're telling me," I said.

"Do you mean to say that you were unable to take a single call off the radio during those two hours?"

"Yes."

"Why?"

"Because my taxicab broke down."

Ottman glanced at the trip-sheet. "When did this happen?"

"I would say that it happened about ten minutes after I left the Arapahoe address. I was headed north on Chambers Road when the engine started to lose power."

Ottman glanced at Quigg, then looked back at me.

"Well ... you certainly were lucky you arrived late at the Arapahoe address," Ottman said. "If they hadn't talked their neighbor into driving them to DIA, you would have found yourself in a very awkward and embarrassing position."

My eyes almost popped out of my head.

CHAPTER 13

Let me explain.

Whenever I'm blindsided by reality, my eyes almost pop out of my head. But I have gotten so used to the capricious nature of reality that I always just move on, and brace myself for the next mess. I deliberately try not to think about what might have happened. This is an adjunct to The Positioning Game, which is something a cabbie plays when he has time to waste. But I was just too busy scrambling to make money to think about the fact that thanks to my ineptitude at pouring water from a tin can I had come close to creating a mess so awful that it nearly made my eyes pop out of my head as I sat in Hogan's office.

I envisioned myself driving the impatient fare to DIA only to have my engine start bucking and losing power. I would have had to call the dispatcher and beg for another Rocky driver to get to the gas station as fast as possible. I envisioned the fare growing hysterical. Me too. It was all too much to dwell on.

I looked at Ottman and began to understand why he was a detective and I wasn't.

"I guess that was a bit of luck after all," I said.

"In all probability they would have missed their flight."

I nodded.

Ottman was being kind to me when he said "probability." I would have said "certainty" but why split hairs?

"What was wrong with your taxi?"

My shoulders drooped. I took a minute to explain the business with the water. At any moment I expected to hear a hideous sound come from Hogan. Nothing came.

"So you were able to get back out on the road as soon as they filled the radiator?"

"Yes."

"Where did you go then?"

"I ate a hamburger at a MacDonald's. After I finished lunch, I drove to the Glendale Bank & Trust and cashed the check given to me by the woman I had driven to Dagwell's."

"Why did you choose to do that rather than, say, deposit it in your own bank?"

"Because I don't trust …" I started to say "people" but instead I said, "… checks."

"Why is that?"

At this point Hogan interrupted.

"Excuse me gentlemen. May I be allowed to say something here?"

"Go right ahead," Ottman said.

"It's not unusual for a taxi driver to cash a check at the earliest opportunity. Drivers are not required to accept checks from customers. It's a judgment call that's left up to the individual driver. But basically it comes down to the fact that sometimes fares write bad checks, and it's best to take a check to the customer's bank and as soon as possible."

I was glad Hogan explained it so diplomatically. I hate to say bad things about customers in front of customers. Even cops take cabs.

"I understand," Ottman said. "All right. You went to the Glendale Bank & Trust and cashed the check, and the check was good. Is that correct?"

"Yes."

"And then what happened?"

I started to roll my eyes and sigh, but instead I said, "That's where my witness statement comes in. I wrote down all the things that …"

I stopped abruptly.

"All the things that … what?" Ottman said.

I swallowed hard.

"All the things that happened from the moment I bumped into the man at the bank until the moment I found myself k …" I managed not to say "kissing the asphalt." I avoided it by turning the letter K into the letter C, as follows: "myself k … coming to a halt along Thirteenth Avenue after I saw the police cars approaching me from behind with their red lights flashing."

I made the sentence extra long so I could get as far away from the letter K as possible.

But here's the thing. The reason I stopped abruptly after saying "I wrote down all the things that …" was because I suddenly realized I had forgotten to tell the police about the five-dollar bill while writing my witness statement. I had intended to do that, but I had forgotten. And now I remembered.

This annoyed me. I wondered if it would annoy the police. I thought about mentioning it right then. This is a problem I have. It's similar to clipping a hangnail. When some little thing bothers me, I have an urge that borders on a psychotic craving to remove it from my life. This is true of big things, too. But I decided to hold off mentioning it because I had learned that the things that bother me don't always bother normal people. Which is to say, I might have been blowing things out of proportion, and I have found that sometimes it is best to do nothing. If you do have to do something, it's always waiting for you anyway. I guess you could call this a "wait-and-see" attitude, except my attitude is "wait-forever."

Detective Ottman made a few last jots on the trip-sheet, then picked it up and looked it over. He turned it around and showed it to me. He held it vertically so that I could see it clearly.

"Now tell me, Murph," he said. "If you had obeyed PUC regulations and filled out your trip-sheet properly, is this how it would have looked?"

I gave the sheet only a cursory glance. I knew that he knew that I knew it was a rhetorical question. The only real question now was whether I was going to play his little mind-game. "Yes," I said.

He set the sheet of paper on Hogan's desk, then looked at me. "All right, Murph, I think I have a clear picture of what you did yesterday. Now I would like you to describe to me in as much detail as possible what you did this morning after you signed out your taxi."

I realized I hadn't "gotten away" with anything. To my knowledge, I have never gotten away with anything ever. This led me to think about the five-dollar bill. But then I had an idea. Why not just explain to these cops that I had intended to mention the fiver, and that I only remembered it a few minutes ago. This would dovetail neatly with my narrative concerning what I had done this morning. It would not only be a part of my story, it would also be true.

I got sort of excited about telling the truth to the police. I mean, I always tell the truth to the police, but this seemed like an "extra-truth" because it sort of had the appearance of a sneaky lie but wasn't. They could have wired me to a lie detector and I would have aced the test. That's how excited I felt. I wanted to race through the business with the penny lady just so I could get to the exciting part, but I had enough experiences with interrogation to know that I'd better take it slowly, and then savor the moment when I got to tell them about remembering the five-dollar bill.

"Okay," I began. "Last night I started thinking that I had been taken advantage of by this Mrs. Jacobs. Plus, I had made no money yesterday, so I decided that I would go back to Mrs. Jacobs' house and ask her to pay me the eight dollars. I felt that this would help to make me feel better."

I paused to let Ottman ask me the sorts of questions that Duncan and Argyle often asked during the middle of my bland narratives. But Ottman just sat and listened.

"So right after putting gas in my taxi this morning, I drove to her

house and knocked on her door. When she came to the door I reintro-
duced myself and asked her to pay me the eight dollars."

"Did she pay you?" Duncan sa … I mean Ottman said.

"No. She refused."

"On what grounds?"

I came to a fork in the road. I didn't want to travel down one of the
tines—the one that would make me look bad, i.e., the bent one. But I
decided to go ahead and do it, since I was suspected of assault and maybe
battery.

"She told me that she didn't owe me any money because I had turned
down the eight hundred pennies on the previous day."

"Pennies are not considered legal tender," Quigg said, while at the
same time continuing to skritch.

I was impressed by that. I can't do two of anything at once. I blame
Newtonian physics.

"That might be a point in your favor," Ottman said.

"Might? How about definitely?"

That's what I wanted to say.

But I decided to hold off. I still had a few more truths in my bag of
surprises.

"I knew that," I said. "But the thing is, I became so frustrated on
Monday when she tried to give me coins that I just said 'Keep your pennies' and I turned and walked away. I got into my cab and drove off. So
basically I turned the money down. What I'm trying to say here is that
I now feel that I did not have a right to go back to her house this morning and demand payment. Our contractual relationship had been dis-
solved by me." I paused a moment, then said, "I've seen *The Paper Chase*
five times."

"But you walked away from pennies," Quigg said. "From a legal
standpoint, it might be said that you walked away from nothing."

"Excuse me," Ottman said, smiling at his partner. "It's true that

Murph walked away from pennies, but he did walk away. A good prosecuting attorney might be able to introduce the idea of 'intent' to a jury."

"What's this about a prosecuting attorney?" I said so quickly that I hardly recognized my voice. I sounded like a chipmunk.

"I'm just speaking hypothetically," Ottman said, turning back to me. "The fact that you walked away from the payment might be viewed as the termination of the implied contract."

"That's what I was getting at," I said.

"A good defense lawyer could make mincemeat out of that argument," Quigg said with a smile. Quigg seemed to be on my side. I didn't like that.

"What I mean is," I said before anybody started measuring me for prison greens, "I felt that I had been in the wrong to return to her house in the first place. Especially after she slammed the door in my face. It sort of woke me up."

"She slammed it?" Quigg said.

"Well ... she closed it abruptly. It made a loud sound. I don't know at what point on the decibel scale an abrupt shut qualifies as a slam, but I will say this ... the sound of the door hitting the frame implied a termination of our conversation."

Ottman and Quigg glanced at each other. Duncan and Argyle used to do that a lot. It always struck me as sort of unprofessional. I mean, it would be obvious to any suspect that the cops were "communicating" with each other when they did it. To take this construct a bit further, it would be obvious to a suspect that a glance between two policemen would be the result of a significant statement made by the suspect, probably an incriminating statement. Ergo, why would the police want to "let on" that the suspect was incriminating himself? Why not remain perfectly motionless and give the suspect enough rope to hang himself? This is one of the many reasons why I frequently remain perfectly motionless. Of course there are others reasons, which I am not at liberty to divulge.

Anyway, it was obvious to me that Ottman and Quigg thought I was as guilty as hell. Of what, I wasn't sure, but by then it seemed irrelevant.

"At any point during your conversation with Mrs. Jacobs did you threaten her?" Ottman said.

"No!" I said.

I stared Ottman in the eye.

"Wait," I said. "Maybe I did."

Ottman remained perfectly motionless. I didn't like that.

"What I mean is, I told her that if she didn't pay me I might have to call the police."

Glance.

I hope I don't have to explain that to you.

"But I wasn't really threatening her," I said. "I mean, I suppose that the threat of … I mean the …" I paused. "I'm trying to think of a synonym for 'threat' that doesn't mean 'threat'."

"How about 'possibility'?" Quigg said.

"Or 'caveat'?" Ottman said.

"Yes, like that," I said. "I suppose the possible caveat of a visit from the police might be considered a threat, but I was just trying to get her to pay me."

I sighed.

"I wasn't thinking clearly. I finally realized I shouldn't have gone there. It's not like me to go around harassing old ladies, or young ladies, or any ladies at all. I guess I was just motivated by the fact that my life seemed to be going to hell in a hatbox."

"Did you say or do anything that might have made Mrs. Jacobs believe you were going to threaten her physically?"

"No. But like I said, I'm not a mind-reader. I don't know how she might have interpreted anything I said or did."

"She told us that you threatened to hit her."

I stared at Ottman for what I estimated to be five thousand years. Then I said, "She lied to you."

"Why would she lie, Murph?"

"Because she's wicked and evil," I wanted to say.

But instead I said, "Why would she try to pay me with eight hundred pennies? Why do old people do any of the strange things they do?" I shrugged. "Maybe she's senile." Or maybe she's a modern-day Morgan La Fay!!!

"So you did not threaten to hit her if she did not pay you?"

"No."

"But you did threaten to call the police."

"Yes."

"Why didn't you call the police?"

"Because I decided it was wrong of me to harass a woman old enough to have played hopscotch wi … back in the nineteen-twenties."

Glance.

"But you could have called the police, correct?"

"Yes."

"And in all probability the police would have made the woman pay."

"I know they would have. They always do."

"Has this happened to you before?"

"Yes."

"When?"

"It happened a couple times after I first started driving."

"What were the situations?"

"They were sort of similar. Except the people who wouldn't pay me were young men. One of the men got out of my cab and walked into a bar. The other man was living at a motel. They were both drunk out of their skulls. Those were the only times I called the police on no-pays."

"Did no-pays happen at any other times?"

"Yes."

"And you didn't call the police?"

"No."

"Why not?"

"Because it took too long for the police to arrive and make the men pay up. I can earn more money by just going on about my business and picking up new fares. I haven't called the police on no-pays in more than twelve years."

"So you have never called the police on anybody aside from those two men?"

"No."

"Not even threatened?"

"No."

"Why didn't you at least threaten to do it?"

"Because some things in life just aren't worth it. It's a judgment call. The times I called the police it was more for the principle of the thing than the money. I didn't like getting ripped off. But I finally decided that money was more important than principle, so I just stopped calling the police and jumped some more bells."

"But you did threaten to call the police on Mrs. Jacobs."

"Yes."

"Was it for the principle of the thing?"

"It was a combination of greed and justice. I wanted the eight dollars, and I figured she was just trying to pull a fast one."

"And that's what made you decide to go to her house and ask for the money?"

"No."

"What do you mean?"

"The reason I decided to go to her house and get the money was because I realized I might have died when the bank robber was in my backseat. I decided that life is too short to let people walk all over me. Just because I'm a cab driver doesn't mean I'm not human. If Mrs. Jacobs had been a thirty-year-old man I might have ended up calling the meat wagon to take him to the morgue."

Glance.

"Are you serious, Murph?"

"No. But that's how mad I was when I went to work. It made me mad to think someone had been holding a gun on me and I didn't even know it. I should have known it though. A man once told me that when you drive a cab you should consider every fare to be armed and dangerous, and be prepared for anything at all times."

"What man?"

"Just a driver I talked to a long time ago. He was an old pro." His name was Big Al. It still is. But I wasn't going to tell the police his name. I would not in my wildest opium-induced nightmares drag Big Al into this. I would let that happen naturally, if it was going to happen at all. I gave it a 1 percent chance of probability, and that was highballing it.

CHAPTER 14

"Can I ask you gentlemen a question?" I said.

"Certainly, Murph," Ottman said.

"What exactly did Mrs. Jacobs tell you?"

Ottman looked up at Quigg, who was holding his pen poised over the notebook. I could tell the cops were communicating. But I had no idea what the "content" of their communication was, which I guess diminishes somewhat my theory about glancing cops. For all I knew they were thinking it was time to head to a donut shop.

Quigg lowered his notebook. "It's this way, Murph. Mrs. Jacobs called 911 at approximately eight-thirty this morning. The medics arrived and found her lying in the hallway next to her telephone. She appeared to be suffering from cardiac arrest. They brought her to DGH. She told the doctors that she had been assaulted by a taxi driver. We were at the hospital talking to the robbery suspect's doctors. So we were contacted, and we went to see Mrs. Jacobs. She told us that she had been assaulted by the same driver who had given her a ride the previous day. We got in touch with Mr. Hogan here, and he checked with the dispatcher, who told us that the driver was named Brendan Murphy. So we came here and asked Mr. Hogan to call you in off the road."

"Did the woman say I hit her?"

"No. She told us that you had threatened to hit her if she didn't pay you for yesterday's ride."

"She lied."

"That's why we called you in, Murph. We wanted to get your side of the story. I have to be honest with you, Murph. This is one of those situations where it's her word against yours."

His honesty was unnecessary. I was way ahead of him.

"Did she have a heart attack?" I said.

"She's been in the cardiac ward for about three hours. We haven't gotten a report from the doctors yet."

I felt a glimmer of hope.

You can carve that on my tombstone.

"As soon as we had your name, we came straight here, Murph."

"Am I under arrest?" I said.

"No," Ottman said. "This is just a preliminary investigation. We have to wait until the doctor's report comes in, and we will need to question Mrs. Jacobs further. We weren't able to question her in-depth at the hospital. She was undergoing tests. But I don't suppose I have to tell you that having your name associated with two elderly people who are in the cardiac care unit at DGH is a coincidence of significant import."

I nodded. Way, way ahead.

Ottman stood up. "I want you to understand something, Murph. We appreciate the cooperation and information you gave us yesterday concerning the bank robbery."

That's all he said.

I waited for him to say something else, but he didn't. I looked him in the eye, hoping he might communicate some sort of subtext, but I didn't see anything. I've never been able to read cops' eyes anyway. It's like trying to read Proust.

Quigg folded his notebook and tucked it away. "The robbery suspect is still unconscious," he said. "So we don't actually know what happened to him."

Ottman and Quigg looked at each other. They appeared to be communicating something big, but they didn't speak. Then Ottman looked at me.

"Sorry to have interrupted your working day," he said. "We're finished here. We'll be in touch with you later. Thanks for cooperating, Murph."

"You're welcome."

The two detectives thanked Hogan. Then they left.

I looked at Hogan.

"Well, that's that I guess."

"What do you mean?" he said.

"I'll turn in my trip-sheet and key to Rollo."

"Why?" Hogan said. "You still have eight hours left on your shift."

I just sat there staring at Hogan. This was out of character. Things weren't going according to Standard Operating Procedure. According to SOP, this was the point at which Hogan was supposed to diplomatically tell me that I was suspended until further notice.

"Oh say … as long as you're here, Murph," he said, "I wonder if I could get you to fill out your trip-sheet from yesterday. I figured you were so busy helping the police solve the bank robbery that you must have overlooked the paperwork."

He slid it across the desk toward me. "I gotta run downstairs," he said. "Why don't you just fill it in, and then leave it on my desk?"

He laid a pen beside the sheet, then got up and walked out of the room and shut the door.

I looked at the door for a bit, then turned and looked at the blank trip-sheet. Next to it was the sheet that had been filled out by Detective Ottoman.

I picked up the pen and began copying the information that Ottman had written down. When I finished filling out my Monday trip-sheet, I signed it and set the pen on the desk, then got up and walked out of the room.

I went downstairs and walked past the cage without looking at Rollo. I went outside and walked over to #123 and climbed in and sat behind the steering wheel.

I looked at my wristwatch. It was almost eleven.

I had earned five dollars in four hours.

I had eight more hours to earn one hundred and twenty-five dollars.

125/8 = 15.60

Call it 16.

I had to earn sixteen dollars an hour for the next eight hours. This was one-dollar-an-hour below the minimum set by the average old pro. It could be done, and I knew I could do it. This depressed me. It would be different if I had to earn thirty dollars an hour for the next eight hours. Then I would have a good excuse to throw in the towel and give up. Good excuses are the best kind of excuses. But I didn't have a good excuse. I didn't have any excuse at all, except an unwillingness to go on living. But that's everybody's excuse.

I wasn't everybody though. I was an asphalt warrior.

Drive, he said.

I started the engine, put the shift into gear, and drove out of the parking lot. I turned the Rocky radio on. I wondered if I would ever again find myself sitting in front of a hotel reading and eating. I wondered if I was going to spend the rest of my life actually working.

All of a sudden I wished I was back at Dyna-Plex. I had earned twenty thousand dollars a year when I worked for Dyna-Plex, and I never did a day's work. I just sat at my desk smoking cigarettes and waiting for the last day of the month so I could write a one-thousand-word typescript of a brochure and hand it to my supervisor who would grab it from my hand and say, "Great! You made the deadline!" Then I would go back to my private office and light up a cigarette and wait another twenty-nine days until it was time to go back to work.

By "day's work" I mean a full day's work. It took me only an hour to write the brochure. Ergo, I worked twelve hours per year at Dyna-Plex.

20,000/12 = 1666.66

Let's make it 1667.

I'll admit it. I'm superstitious.

I was earning $1,667.00 an hour at Dyna-Plex. But I had thrown it all away for a hotel, a bell, a Twinkie, and a joe.

I started taking calls off the radio. I worked The Hill. When The Hill went dry, I moved out across the city and into the suburbs. By the end of the day I had averaged nineteen dollars an hour. I wasn't impressed.

I drove back to the motor and arrived at five minutes to seven. I shut off the radio that had been barking at me for eight hours. I signed the trip-sheet. I had filled in the boxes after each drop-off. All the eyes were dotted and all the tees were crossed.

I gathered up my accoutrement and walked into the on-call room. I handed my key and trip-sheet to Rollo. Neither of us said anything. Our Sopwith Camels were grounded. The war was over. I could feel it. Maybe he could, too.

I walked out of the on-call room, got into my heap, and drove back to my crow's nest.

I dropped my accoutrement on the kitchen table, then went into the bedroom and tossed my profits for the day onto the nightstand. I kicked off my Keds, got undressed, crawled under my blanket and went to sleep.

This always happens to me when I work hard.

I slept for more than nine hours.

When I woke up it was five o'clock in the morning, a terrible time to wake up. Too late to go back to sleep and too early to go to work. Who invented five o'clock anyway?

It was Wednesday, my usual day for working. But I wasn't sure I wanted to go to work. Which is to say, I didn't want to work at all, but what's that got to do with my life? Monday had been terrible, and Tuesday had been terrible in a different way, but at least I had made up my Monday losses. And here it was Wednesday and time to do it again. My life was arranged so that I usually worked only every other day, three weeks out of a month, and now I was working three days in a row. I tried to make sense of it all.

Normally my work schedule gets bollixed up when I find myself getting involved in the personal life of a fare. But I hadn't tried to help anybody in a long time. Then something clicked inside my brain. Wait a minute. I did try to help somebody. I tried to help those people down on Arapahoe and Chambers. The dispatcher had been begging a cabbie to take the call, and nobody would take it. So I had decided to jump in and save the day. Sure, greed had played a role in my motivation, but still, I tried to help somebody, and look where it had gotten me.

Right then and there I made a vow that as long as I lived I would never again try to help anybody from Aurora.

I relaxed and gazed idly at the ceiling. The curtain on the window that fronts my headboard, if my bed had a headboard, was parted, and every so often a car would pass on 13th Avenue. The glow of the headlights made abstract shapes on the ceiling. It was like gazing at fast-moving clouds in the sky. A sky made of plaster. Clouds made of light. Darkness made of shadow. It was a pleasant little light show.

Then my eyes almost popped out of my head.

I had forgotten to tell Ottman and Quigg about the five-dollar bill!

"Goddamn it," I snarled.

Why hadn't I remembered to tell them about the fiver? Then I remembered why. I was a suspect in an assault case and my mind had been befuddled. Thank God I had a good excuse. I forgave myself. I rarely do that.

I started thinking about Mrs. Jacobs. I thought terrible things about her. I thought she had taken her penny scam further than she had ever taken it before. I thought she had been ripping off cab drivers for years, and now she saw an opportunity to make some real dough. I thought she was going to sue the Rocky Mountain Taxicab Company for a bundle by filing a bogus assault charge against one of its employees. Except I wasn't an employee, I was an independent contractor. But a good lawyer could make mincemeat out of that fact. The insurance company for Rocky Cab would probably pay her off, and might insist that I do a little hard time in Cañon City.

Her word against mine.

Jaysus.

It was five-thirty a.m. when I finally got out of bed, pulled on my jeans and Keds, and walked into the kitchen to make a pan of scrambled eggs. I rarely do that. I usually eat a cheese sandwich with a soda. Bachelor breakfast. But I hadn't eaten since noon the previous day, not counting Twinkies. I hadn't been hungry when I got home. I just crawled under my blanket and went to sleep. This happens every time the police interrogate me for assault or robbery or kidnapping or murder. It's a psychological tic.

I carried the frying pan full of eggs into the living room. I watched TV while I ate my scrambles and sipped a soda. I channel-surfed in between forkfuls of egg. I was completely out of my element. I hadn't watched morning TV since I was a little kid. But that was long ago, and in smaller shoes.

I surfed the channels for two minutes. That was how long it took to eat breakfast. Afterwards I carried the pan into the kitchen and set it in the sink to soak. I decided to go for broke and make a cheese sandwich. I was still hungry. It's a funny thing about eggs. When you scramble five of them, they seem like only three eggs. I probably should have scrambled seven eggs, then it would have seemed like five. I wondered if there was an algebraic formula I could apply to scrambling eggs. I figured algebra must be good for something.

I unwrapped the end of a loaf of bread and pulled out two slices. I reached into the fridge and pulled out a slice of American cheese. I placed the cheese squarely in the center of one piece of bread. I placed the second piece of bread on top of the cheese. I was a regular Wolfgang Puck.

Then I felt something.

My kitchen began to vibrate. I recognized it. Someone was coming up the fire escape. The last time this happened, the vibration was caused by a guy named Harold. He's a bartender at Sweeney's Tavern. I don't want to talk about him.

I stood in the middle of the kitchen with the sandwich in my left hand. I heard a knock on my door.

It was like hearing the sound of a telephone ringing. I hate telephones—especially the ringing part.

"Who's there?" I said.

It occurred to me that I had never said that when answering a telephone. If I had, maybe it would have caused people to stop calling me. People freak out when other people diverge from accepted social protocols. Except I didn't have that problem anymore. I owned a telephone answering machine. I wished like hell I owned a door answering machine.

"Police! Open up!" a voice shouted.

At last—after a lifetime of unexpected surprises—my eyes finally popped out of my head.

"Okay!" I said.

I unbolted the lock and pulled the door open. It was the police all right, and they were dressed for business. Some people call it "S.W.A.T."

They came in fast.

A cop pointed a glove, or a gun, at me. Either way, it was black. "Drop the sandwich and raise your hands!" he said.

I reached for the plaster sky.

CHAPTER 15

I'll never forget the sound of the sandwich hitting the linoleum. It made a kind of "thwup." I had never heard that sound before—and thinking back on it, I realized that in my entire life I had never dropped a sandwich.

There were six uniformed cops, and behind them came Ottman and Quigg. Quigg held up a piece of paper in front of my face. "We have a warrant to search your apartment, Mr. Murphy," he said. "We ask that you cooperate. You have the right to remain silent. Anything you say can be held against you in a court of law."

Now that I was on the receiving end of a monologue from every cop show I had ever seen, it suddenly occurred to me that my Fifth Amendment rights were being violated.

It's funny how you never think those things when you're watching TV. What I mean is, "Anything you say can be held against you in a court of law" seems to run counter to the idea that a person can't be forced to testify against himself. Just because an officer of the law tells you that anything you say can be used against you, does the Bill of Rights go down the crapper? It seemed to me that rather than being told he has the right to remain silent, the cops should force a suspect to remain silent. Gag the sonofabitch if they have to. I wondered how many criminals had been sent up the river just because they accidentally blabbed in front of a cop.

As you might surmise, my brain was having a bit of difficulty dealing with the fact that my crow's nest had been invaded by strangers. This hadn't happened since New Year's Eve eight years back when apparently I invited everyone in Sweeney's over for a nightcap.

"What's this all about, Detective Ottman?" I said, taking a cavalier attitude toward my right to remain silent.

"Mr. Murphy, we have reason to believe that you are in possession of the money that was stolen from the Glendale Bank & Trust."

The words were barely out of his mouth when I did something over which I had no control. I chortled. Even as I was trying to make sense out of his assertion, my throat was laughing. Not a boisterous deep-bellied laugh, but more like a staccato burp. I've had this problem all my life. It always seems to be associated with the truth, or more precisely, the lack of truth. Maybe I've been subconsciously programmed to respond to un-truths the way most people respond to whoopee cushions. When I know for a fact that something isn't true and I see people running around acting upon a lie as if it were true, I laugh. Some people become outraged. Some people roll their eyes with disdain—Oscar Wilde comes to mind. I, on the other hand, chortle.

"I'm afraid we are going to have to take you down to police head-quarters, Mr. Murphy. Things will be clarified for you there. But right now we are going to search your apartment. I would like to ask you to finish getting dressed. Then Officer Quigg is going to escort you down the stairs and place you into the rear of our vehicle. We would be grateful for your cooperation, Mr. Murphy."

I wanted to ask if they were going to put the cuffs on me. You may not believe this, but I have never been handcuffed by a policeman in my life.

Quigg followed me through the living room where the uniformed men were carefully poking around in my stuff. One of them lifted a chair cushion revealing a VCR remote-control device. "So that's where it went!" I exclaimed. I glanced at Quigg. "After I lost it I went to Radio Shack and bought one of those remotes that you have to program your-self. Jeez what a bag of snakes."

Quigg didn't blink. He followed me into my bedroom where the po-
lice were snooping around. I put on my T-shirt. It was a nice day out, so
I didn't bother getting a jacket. I grabbed my billfold off the nightstand.
"Do you need to search this before I put it in my back pocket?"

Quigg nodded. I handed it over.

He opened it and looked inside. It was empty but for my driver's
license and a credit card.

"*You* have a credit card?" he said.

I could tell right away he regretted putting his emphasis on the word
You. But I understood. "Yes," I said. "I got it when I was in college. My
Maw co-signed for it. The credit limit was two hundred dollars. But I
only use it when I rent cars."

"Do you rent cars very often?"

"No."

"Can I ask you the last time you rented a car using this credit card?"

"Yes."

"When was it?"

"When I flew out to Los Angeles awhile back to save a gi … to try
and sell a screenplay about surfing beach bunnies."

He closed the billfold and handed it back.

I tucked it into my pocket. "My credit's up to three hundred dollars
now," I said. It had the quality of a non sequitur. He ignored it.

As we walked toward the bedroom door I glanced at a corner and
noticed a cop opening the lid of my steamer trunk. I stopped walking.
It was like a chortle. I had no control over it. "Does he have to look in
there?" I said.

Everybody stopped what they were doing and looked at me.

"What's the problem, Mr. Murphy?" Quigg said.

My shoulders drooped. "There's no problem, I guess."

"It sounds like you have a problem with my man searching that
trunk," Quigg said.

I shook my head. "No, it's okay."

"Mr. Murphy, do you have any weapons in this apartment?"

"You mean like swords?"

"I mean guns."

"Oh … no. I haven't touched a gun in years."

"When was the last time you touched a gun?"

"The day before I got discharged from the army. My sergeant made me clean my rifle. It was ridiculous. We had an inspection two days earlier but he made me clean it again before I could go home. He sent me to the barbershop, too. I think he was out to get me."

"Mr. Murphy, is there anything in the steamer trunk that you don't want us to see?"

"Yes."

"What?"

"Novels."

"Pornographic novels?"

"Rejected novels."

"Mr. Murphy, could I ask you to be less obtuse when you answer my questions?"

"Yes."

"What sort of novels are you talking about?"

"Novels that I wrote and sent to publishers. They got sent back with rejection slips. There's about a hundred of them in there. The rejection slips are attached to the first page of each manuscript." I hung my head. "I know you're not supposed to collect rejection slips. That's what the how-to books say anyway. But it's the only proof I have that anybody in New York City even touched them. They make me feel sort of good."

"All right, men, continue the search," Quigg said. "Let's go outside, Mr. Murphy."

I desperately wanted him to stop calling me Mr. Murphy. It created an image in my mind of Mister Greenjeans being led out of the Treasure

House in handcuffs. I saw Captain Kangaroo lying in a crumpled heap in front of Grandfather Clock. Bunny Rabbit was weeping. It was unbearable. But I kept my mouth shut. I figured I had already said too much. I wished I hadn't mentioned the how-to books. I don't like people to know that I don't know how-to write novels.

Quigg didn't cuff me though, which was a good thing. I thought a lot about that as I made my way down the fire escape, which is about as steep as man-made things ever get. Douglas Fairbanks might have been able to walk down with his hands cuffed behind his back—he probably would have slid down the railing and thrown in a couple of somersaults. I did that one New Year's Eve without any acting lessons.

Quigg put me into the backseat of his unmarked cruiser. I felt foolish. I felt like everybody in the neighborhood who had a window was looking at me. I always feel like this though. I blame nuns. When I was in sixth grade I once stood on top of my desk after the nun left the room, and when I looked at the door, she was watching me through the window. It gave me a psychological tic.

There were four police cars crowding the parking lot behind my apartment building. I prayed that none of the other tenants would come home. They get crabby if their parking spaces are blocked. I don't blame them. I myself am pretty territorial when it comes to parking spaces, toys, and barstools.

It took about half an hour for the police to search my apartment. You might think I would have felt like I was being "violated" by the unexpected scrutiny of my personal belongings, but I had one thing going for me: I own nothing.

By "nothing" I mean "practically nothing." In a way I felt sorry for the cops when they came out empty-handed because I had the funny feeling they felt sorry for me.

Naturally I knew that they wouldn't find the stolen money in my possession. It made me feel like I had gotten hold of the answers to a pop-quiz in high school. I was going to ace another test. But I tried not to think about all the unpublished novels that they saw, which included a bookshelf built entirely out of novels so badly written that I would never send them to a publisher again. I used them in the way that normal people use bricks. One thing did make me feel uneasy though: I had told the police that the steamer trunk was full of rejected novels, but half of the manuscripts were rejected screenplays. A street-smart cop just might notice the variation in typescript formatting, and wonder what else I was lying about.

I watched as the last of the policemen came trooping down the fire escape with the forlorn expressions that you often see on the faces of people who are acquainted with unpublished writers. They gathered around Ottman and Quigg and spoke for a few minutes, some of them whispering secrets to their shoulders. Then they got into their patrol cars and drove out of the lot. One cop glanced at me, but he quickly looked away. I knew what he was thinking: form rejections. There wasn't a single handwritten rejection slip in my trunk.

Quigg opened the rear door and asked me to step out. I emerged feeling refreshed. To an innocent man, thirty minutes in the rear of a cop car is like twenty minutes of Transcendental Meditation.

"We're going to take you down to headquarters for further questioning, Mr. Murphy. But first I'd like to ask you to go upstairs and secure your apartment. I'll come with you."

I walked up the stairs trying to keep a smug smirk off my face. After we stepped inside I asked him if it was okay if I policed up my fallen sandwich. I said "policed" on purpose. I was being ironic. It was probably good he didn't notice. The only thing I have more trouble with than my chortling is my English degree.

I closed up shop and went back downstairs with Quigg. I was again placed in the backseat. Ottman drove. I took what I had begun to think of as "The Ride." As I said, I had done this before but so far I had managed to avoid actually being arrested. From what little I knew about odds though, I suspected my number was up. I had been accused of threatening an old lady, and I was suspected of possessing money stolen during the commission of a felony. In both cases there were victims old enough to be my grandparents. If this was a cop show I'd be rooting for the hangman.

We rolled down into the DPD basement. I knew the routine. I led Ottman and Quigg up to the Robbery Division and let myself into a small room. I took a seat at a table and invited them to sit down. "Before we get started, gentlemen," I said, "I have one favor I'd like to ask."

"What is it, Mr. Murphy?" Ottman said.

"Could you please call me Murph?"

"All right, Murph. This morning around four a.m. the robbery suspect regained consciousness. The nurse informed the guards at the door. One of the guards contacted us while the other remained at the man's side. The man spoke to him briefly. By the time we got there, the man had lost consciousness again. We were not able to question him, but the guard did get some information out of him. The man identified himself as Carlton Hollister. We already knew this. When he was found unconscious in the parking lot he had a briefcase with him and he had a billfold that contained his driver's license. The billfold also contained some money. The only thing missing was the money he had stolen from the bank. The teller whom he robbed was able to identify him from a photograph."

I pursed my lips and nodded. I didn't really have to do this, but I felt sort of foolish just staring at Ottman as if I was watching a TV show. Sometimes when I watch TV I purse my lips and nod, usually when the lottery numbers don't match the numbers on the tickets I secretly buy.

"The man was conscious long enough to confess that he had, in fact, robbed the Glendale Bank & Trust."

I stopped nodding.

"But when we opened his briefcase we found it empty."

I stopped nodding even more, which is not a scientific impossibility, because I did it.

CHAPTER 16

Ottman and Quigg stared at me. I stared right back. That's one thing about myself that I've always taken pride in: whenever I tell the truth I don't feel the least bit flustered. I only get flustered when I lie. I don't mean lying to cops but the people that any average person lies to on a daily basis in order to keep from being pestered with further conversation. It's hard to keep track of all the lies though, especially when you get repeat customers in your cab. You can never remember what the hell kind of malarkey you said to your fare two weeks ago in an attempt to increase the size of your tip. But anybody who lies to a cop is living in a fool's paradise.

"I have another question for you, Murph," Ottman said.

"Shoot."

"You told us that prior to driving Mr. Hollister to his office, you had seen him before. You said he was standing directly behind you when you were in the bank cashing the check from the sales lady at Dagwell's."

"That's right."

"Had you ever seen Mr. Hollister prior to that?"

"No."

"Are you sure?"

"Yes."

"Is it possible that he had been a fare in your taxi and that you simply didn't remember him?"

"Yes."

"Why do you say that?"

"Because it's true. The backseat of my taxi is like Grand Central Station. I hardly remember anybody who rides in the backseat unless it's a particularly memorable person."

"What kind of person might that be?"

"Just somebody who does something that I might remember."

"Could you give us an example?"

"Well ... one time a guy got into my backseat with a TV. I mean, he put the TV in my trunk, and then we drove to a pawnshop where he sold it. I'll never forget that. It broke my heart."

"Why?"

"Because I don't like people to not have TVs."

"That strikes me as a strange attitude for someone who writes novels. I thought all novelists hated television."

"Well, I'm not published. Maybe if I get published I'll start hating television. I don't know. I'll just have to wing it."

"Murph, after Mr. Hollister got out of your taxi, did you notice if he was approached by anyone?"

"No."

"Why not?"

"After people get out of my taxi I don't look at them."

"Why not?"

"Because I've got their money."

"What if it's a beautiful woman?"

"I suppose that during the past fourteen years I might have looked at a beautiful woman after she got out of my taxi. But I'm just saying that I make a habit of forgetting everybody I meet as quickly as possible."

There was a knock at the door.

Quigg got up from the table and walked over to the door. Somebody's hand appeared in the doorway and gave Quigg a large manila envelope. There was a whispered conversation. One-sided. Quigg merely nodded. I guess that qualifies as a conversation. He took the envelope and shut the door. I think it was a woman's hand. It was little.

Quigg sat back down at the table and looked at Ottman. He nodded. Quigg opened the envelope and pulled out a five-dollar bill wrapped in cellophane. He set it on the table in front of me.

"Do you recognize this five-dollar bill?" he said.

"No."

"Let me refresh your memory, Murph. During the search of your apartment we found this five-dollar bill hidden between the pages of a Bible."

"Oh that five-dollar bill," I said.

I sat back in my chair and slapped the tabletop. "You're not going to believe this," I said, chuckling lightly, "but I was going to tell you about that fiver. In fact I was going to mention it in my witness statement, only I forgot. Then I was going to tell you about it yesterday, and once again I forgot. I couldn't believe it."

Glance.

"Can I ask you a question, Murph?"

Ottman kept asking me if he could ask me questions. I finally pegged this as a subtle interrogation technique designed to throw me off-balance. I found it hard to believe that a man would keep saying it during an interrogation and so would anybody else with half a brain. Duncan and Argyle used to pull that on me, too. It would have gotten annoying if I wasn't the kind of person who is amused by obvious ploys.

Lay it on me," I said.

"When did you first come into possession of this money?"

"Right after the bank robbery. But the thing is, gentlemen, I completely forgot about it until it came time to mention it in my witness statement. I thought it might be part of the stolen loot, ya know? But then, wouldn't you know it, I forgot to write it down. This happens to me a lot when I write fiction. I get some idea that I want to elaborate on, but then I get so fixated by some other part of my story that I completely forget to mention the very thing that made me sit down to start writing the story in the first place. I once wrote a story that didn't even have a plot if you can believe that."

They waited for me to finish talking. When it looked like I was finished, Ottman said, "So when we spoke to you yesterday, you intended to tell us about this, but you forgot again, is that correct?"

"Yes. Well. But that was before I found out that I was a suspect in an assault. That completely made me forget about the matter of the five dollars. And then when I woke up this morning I suddenly remembered that I had forgotten to mention it, and it just irritated the heck out of me."

"Let me ask you something, Murph," Quigg said, resting his elbows on the table and clasping his hands together. "Did you have any intention of telling us about this five-dollar bill today?"

"No."

"Why not?"

"I forgot again. I didn't even think about it until just now when you showed it to me. I guess having the S.W.A.T. team raid my house was like getting charged with assault. The five bucks sort of got shunted to the rear of my mind."

"So you believe that this money was stolen from the bank?" he said.

"Well of course. I mean … wasn't it?"

All of a sudden I felt off-balance.

"We didn't say it was, Murph."

I didn't chortle this time. I just blew air out of my mouth with amusement, which made my lips flap. "I didn't know if it actually was a part of the stolen money. I just thought it might be. That's why I was going to tell you about it. It seemed relevant."

The room grew silent.

I swallowed hard.

"Can I ask you gentlemen something?" I said.

"Yes," Ottman said.

"Is that five-dollar bill a part of the stolen money?"

"Yes."

I took a deep breath and blew a sigh of relief. "Well, I'm glad I cleared that up."

"Could you clear up something else for us, Murph?" Ottman said.

"Sure."

"Can you tell us where you got this five-dollar bill?"

"Oh. I thought I explained that."

"No," he said. "You didn't."

"I thought I did."

"Why don't you explain it again."

"Okay. Mr. Hollister paid me with it at the end of the cab ride. The fare came to about two dollars, and he gave me the five and told me to keep it."

Ottman frowned. "Didn't it strike you as odd that a man would give you a three-dollar tip on a two-dollar ride?"

"Not really."

"Why not?"

"It happens rather frequently. Businessmen are good tippers. I sometimes think businessmen feel sorry for cab drivers, so they give us big tips."

"What makes you think they feel sorry for you?"

"Because it happens so often. Pity is the only explanation I've ever come up with."

Quigg nodded. So did Ottman. I tried not to interpret their nods. As familiar as I am with body language translated into spoken English, it's still not an exact science.

"We matched the serial number of this five-dollar bill with that of the stolen money," Ottman said. "It came from a brand-new stack of fives that the teller had placed in the drawer that morning."

I nodded. I hoped they didn't try to interpret the nod, because whatever they might have thought I meant by it, they would have been wrong. It meant nothing. I was just nodding.

"We obtained the warrant to search your apartment, Murph, because we suspected you may have come into possession of the stolen money. After we took the briefcase to the bank, the teller identified it as the briefcase into which the robber had placed the money. But as I told you, when we opened it, we found it empty."

He paused a moment to let this sink in.

It did.

"Mr. Hollister was found lying unconscious in the parking lot by a woman who was returning to work from lunch," he said. "She called an ambulance, and Mr. Hollister was taken to Denver General Hospital. The doctors determined that he had suffered a heart attack. It took us a while to connect the man with the robbery. There was a lot of radio activity that afternoon. When a report came in that a man fitting the description of the robber had been taken to DGH at the same time we were looking for the man, we were able to link him up. He was carrying a gun, he had his identification on him, but he did not have the stolen money."

I started nodding, but I was actually thinking. I guess you could say I was "buying time" with the nod while my mind was racing. "Maybe after he got out of my cab he was robbed in the parking lot. That would explain it."

"You're right," Ottman said. "That would explain it."

"Or maybe he handed the money to a friend who quickly drove off in a getaway car, and then Mr. Hollister had a heart attack. That would explain it."

"You're right," Ottman said. "That would explain it, too."

I felt like a screenwriter pitching a cop show. I tried to come up with some more convenient explanations. I was amazed at how easy resolving a conflict could be if you just gave it some thought. That might turn out to be a technique I could apply to writing novels.

"Maybe you could explain something else for us, Murph," Ottman said. He picked up the five-dollar bill and held it up for me to see. "Why do you keep money hidden in a Bible?"

"It seems like a good place to hide money," I said. "I've always felt that a burglar would feel too guilty to rifle a Bible in search of money."

"Why do you think that?"

"It's sort of a combination of inductive logic and faith. Nobody has ever stolen anything from my Bible before, so I just keep hiding money there."

Quigg frowned. "Murph, we also found money hidden in a copy of a book called *Lolita*."

I nodded.

"Do you think a burglar would feel guilty rifling *Lolita*?"

"No. But *Lolita* is a work of literary fiction. I don't think the average burglar rifles literature."

"Has it ever been tampered with by a burglar?"

"No, but my friends used to steal the book itself."

"What friends?"

"English majors. Whenever I had a party with my college buddies, my copy of *Lolita* would disappear. Then I would buy another one."

"So why do you keep putting money in it?"

"Because I don't let my friends come over anymore."

"Why not?"

"Because they kept stealing *Lolita*."

"Why did they keep stealing *Lolita*?"

"I think they were too embarrassed to buy it."

"But you're not?"

"Nah. I'm more embarrassed to buy spy thrillers. I have a degree in English so I feel like a dimwit when I buy spy thrillers."

"I enjoy reading spy thrillers," Quigg said.

"Me too," I said. "That's why I buy them. That's also why I write them."

"Have you ever gotten any of them published?"

"No."

"Do you know anything about spying?"

"No."

"Don't they say that you should write only what you know about?"

"Yeah. But they say a lot of things. I generally ignore advice from people who don't give me money."

"Maybe they would give you money if you listened to their advice."

That stopped me cold.

"How long have you been writing unpublished novels, Murph?"

"About twenty years."

"You don't earn much money as a cab driver, do you?"

"Not hardly. I sort of live from hand-to-mouth."

"Do you hope to make money off your writing?"

"Yes."

Glance.

"Most writers wouldn't admit that," Quigg said.

"I know. But I'm not like most writers, except for the not getting paid part. I do have that in common with people who don't write for money."

"How long have you been driving a taxi, Murph?"

"Fourteen years."

"That's a long time to live from hand-to-mouth."

"You're telling me."

"What would you do if you came into a lot of money, Murph?"

I laughed. "The first thing I would do is quit cab driving and hop a plane to Tahiti."

Ottman and Quigg looked at each other, and it wasn't just a glance. They were definitely communicating. I stopped laughing.

"But I do realize," I said, clearing my throat, "that a first novelist is lucky to get two or three thousand dollars for an advance on a book. So I don't actually expect to come into a lot of money any time soon."

Quigg raised his chin, and simultaneously frowned and looked down at the tabletop. This is what people do who are at the tail end of sorting out their thoughts. I can always see it coming.

"Murph," he said, "I wonder if you could describe for us exactly what you did from the moment you dropped Mr. Hollister off until your taxi was pulled over by the police." He reached into the manila envelope and pulled out a sheet of paper. "I have a copy of your witness statement here. I'm going to use it as a reference."

The statement was fifteen pages long. I had used up all the extra sheets of paper that they had given to me that day.

"You mean you want me to go back over the things I wrote down?"

"Yes," he said. "We have found that witnesses often forget minor though important details when they are asked to write a statement immediately after undergoing a traumatic experience. Take that five dollars, for instance. I think we can agree that it was a minor though significant detail, yet you forgot it. Perhaps there are other details that will come back to you, now that you are not under pressure to write down everything you can recall."

"Well, okay, sure, I can do that, although I would like to say that as someone who has been writing prose fiction all his adult life, he has never … I mean I has never … I mean I have never had difficulty expressing my thoughts."

"Not counting the five dollars."

"Well, yes, but I mean, I'm just saying that the witness statement is not a hodgepodge of rambling sentences. Each and every sentence was well thought-out ahead of time. I mean, you can count on the accuracy of every statement I wrote down."

"I understand."

"Well. Okay. I just wanted to make sure you were aware that as someone who has been writing for a long time I am not like the average chump you drag in off the … I mean, you know, the ordinary person who is an amateur when it comes to focusing his thoughts and then typing them consecutively on sheets of blank paper."

"I understand."

"Well. Okay. I just, you know, wanted to make that clear."

"Yes."

"Well, let's see …" I said.

As I began my narrative, Quigg picked up his copy of my witness statement and looked at it.

I wasn't kidding when I told him that he could count on every statement I had put down. I had written my experiences exactly as I would have described them verbally to a patron at Sweeney's, which meant I had it down pat. I don't know if this qualifies as a memorization trick or what, but when I tell a story, the individual sentences remain in my mind like individual suits hanging on a mobile rack in a dry-cleaning store. Ergo, as I recounted my experiences of that day, I recited virtually a verbal Xerox of what I had written. I knew this because as I spoke, Quigg kept glancing from the witness statement to my lips and back again.

It got to the point where he began silently and apparently unconsciously reading along with me as I spoke. We were like a vaudeville team in a way. I was talking and he was silently lip-synching with me. I didn't know what the point of the act would have been, or whether an audience would have been entertained, but it occurred to me that he could have been a guy who had answered a want-ad for a job as a ventriloquist's dummy. It seemed to me that an act like that might have possibilities for a few "laffs" as they used to say on old Broadway.

When I finished speaking, he looked at me with an expression that I can only describe as "baffled."

"Interesting," he said. "Your spoken narrative matches your written narrative word for word."

I smiled with my lips compressed the way humble people do.

"It's almost as if you had spent weeks memorizing this," he said.

I stopped smiling.

"I never work from memory," I said. "I don't believe in writing auto-biographical fiction. I like making things up."

"Is that a fact?" he said.

I started to say yes, but then I stopped. I thought about what I had just said, and sort of wished I hadn't said it.

"Do you enjoy making up stories, Murph?"

I had heard that question somewhere before. It was something that a creative-writing teacher in college might have said. But then I remembered who had said it. A cop. Specifically, a detective named Duncan. He asked the question in reference to the murder of a homeless man. This struck me as coincidental, and I immediately wondered if Ottman had consulted with him about this case. That didn't seem quite fair. It had the earmarks of a clever trap.

I cleared my throat. "I'm referring to fiction novels about vampires or robots," I said. "Not witness statements to the police. I would never lie to a policeman. I can't imagine anything more risky, and people tell me I've got a pretty lively imagination."

"Maybe you should write a novel about a man who lies to the police," Quigg said.

"That's a thought," I said. And I meant it.

Quigg set the statement on the table and smiled at me. "That was a very impressive performance, Murph," he said. "But during your narrative you left out one detail?"

"What's that?"

"The five-dollar bill."

I smacked my forehead with my palm. "Dang!" I shook my head

with exasperation. "I was going to mention it this time for sure, but then I forgot. I don't know what's the matter with me."

"That's all right, Murph," Quigg said. "We're clear on the five-dollar bill now, so don't worry about it."

I was still shaking my head. You know how you go into the kitchen to get something, but when you get there you forget what you went for? You stand there trying to recall what it was, like Scotch tape or a potato or something, but you can't remember. So you go back into the living room and sit down and pick up your soda and suddenly you say, "Ice! I went to get ice!" but you hadn't brought your glass when you went into the kitchen because you were trying to take a kind of short-cut because you hadn't felt like carrying your glass all the way into ... well anyway, that's how I felt.

"I think we're finished with you for now, Murph," Quigg said.

"Am I going to jail?" I blurted out.

"No. We're going to let you go," Quigg said. "I hope you understand that we had to bring you in after Mr. Hollister made his statement so we could question you further. And we had to search your apartment. We believe your story about the five-dollar bill, Murph. We have no reason to keep you here any longer. We know we inconvenienced you, but we do hope you understand."

I knew that I was expected to smile and nod and say I understood, but instead I said, "Can you tell me how much money was stolen from the bank?"

Glance.

Ottman smiled. "It's going to end up in the paper, if it's not already there," he said. "The robber got in the neighborhood of one-hundred thousand dollars."

It took all my willpower not to utter a punch line as old as vaudeville. But my eyes did get big, and completely on their own. I had never been that close to that much money in my whole life, not counting Monday.

I felt like I was getting all hot and sweaty, like I did when I learned that the robber had been carrying a gun. Guns and money—the tools of the rich and dangerous. I felt a psychological tic coming on.

Before I was allowed to leave, they asked me to sign a piece of paper that amounted to a receipt for the five-dollar bill that they had taken from my apartment. It had been identified as stolen money. They didn't offer to replace it with a "clean" fiver, but I didn't press the issue. I'm sure an expensive lawyer could have forced the government to replace it. Who says you can't buy justice? I've never heard a lawyer say it and I've spoken to plenty of lawyers, believe me.

CHAPTER 17

I t was nine a.m. when I got back home. A street patrolman in a black-and-white chauffeured me. The Denver Police Department doesn't actually use black-and-white cars. They're blue-and-white, but it's just easier for me to say black-and-white because everybody knows what that means and it saves me from having to make long-winded explanations every time I get hauled in.

I guess I don't have to tell you that I was feeling sort of "wrung out" by then. Ottman and Quigg told me that the charges laid on me by Mrs. Jacobs were still pending. She was in the cardiac unit undergoing tests. It was still her word against mine. Her lawyer had arranged that the investigation be put on hold until she was given the green light by her doctors to talk to the police. Detective Quigg advised me to get a lawyer. He might as well have advised me to get a dentist. I didn't have any money for a lawyer. It looked like I was scheduled to play the lead role in *Gideon's Trumpet* once again. Thank God for Henry Fonda. At least nowadays an innocent man has a chance of going to jail with a reduced sentence.

As I stated before my apartment got ransacked, this was Wednesday, my normal day for work. I knew I had to go in, get a cab, and pull at least a short-shift. This meant I would earn either twenty-five dollars, or else fifty dollars. I could do both. But it's hard to work hard when you're wrung out. I didn't feel like doing anything except starting my life over. But that would entail a trip to Wichita. That was out of the question. I had pulled eighteen years of hard time in Wichita. After I got out of the army I was sent back to "The Big W" for two more years. But I finally escaped, although I didn't think of it as escape. I was just angry, so I left. They don't let you do that in the army.

But I left Wichita because I had asked a girl to marry me and she turned me down. Also, I was fed up with college. I just wanted to be a novelist. I was tired of studying books. I wanted to write them. I figured the time had come to go out into the real world and get some experiences that I could turn into novels. I know this sounds contradictory to what I told Quigg, but it's not. I planned on using my experiences and insights as a basis for characters in science-fiction novels. I was a fan of Robert Heinlein in those days. I wanted to write a novel about a teenager who lives on Mars. He gets fed up with Mars and travels to other planets. That's about as far as I got with the plot. I had hoped that by the time I got to Los Angeles, the teenager would be on Jupiter. Since LA is the biggest city in America, I assumed that whatever happened to me in LA would happen to the teenager on the biggest planet in the solar system. I got a job delivering ice cream. Let's move on.

I decided to call Rocky Cab and see if #123 had been signed out by someone else. The fact that I hadn't shown up by seven-thirty meant that Rollo might have leased the cab to another driver, and had done so with relish. He knew that I normally drove on Wednesday, and he also knew I was having legal problems. If the cab was signed out, I would be forced to lease one of the clunkers that Rocky Cab keeps around for newbies who can't decide whether to go full-time on a weekly lease with a decent cab, or stick with part-time driving like me. I was the oldest part-time driver at Rocky Cab. I had been driving part-time for fourteen years because I had always believed that I would one day sell a novel, and if I sold one I didn't want to get stuck finishing out a weekly lease. I mean, why would a guy with a million dollars spend a few extra days driving a taxi? I wanted to keep my options open.

I sat down in my easy chair next to my telephone. But instead of picking up the phone and dialing Rocky, I picked up my remote and turned on the TV. I was psychologically working my way toward the telephone. I wanted to speak to Rollo even less than I wanted to die.

I tried channel surfing but I couldn't get into it because I knew I was just pretending to watch TV. It felt "wrong." I finally switched it off and picked up the phone and dialed the cage.

"Rocky Cab," Rollo said.

His voice sort of made me laugh. He sounded like a duck. Everybody sounds like a duck on the phone. You would think that an invention as old as the telephone would have undergone some acoustical upgrades since the day Alexander Graham Bell quacked, "Watson, come here, I want you."

I told Rollo I wanted to come in and pick up a cab for a short-shift, and asked if 123 was available. He said it was. Had this been a Monday or a Friday, the busy days, 123 probably would have been leased to a newbie. But nobody had driven 123 that day. I then asked if I would be able to lease it until seven o'clock, and he told me yes.

I would be leasing it on an hourly rate. Short-shifts are normally six hours, and full-shifts are twelve hours, but Rocky Cab is more than willing to squeeze every last nickel out of its drivers any way possible. This worked in my favor because I would be able to pull a nine-hour shift if I got down to Rocky right away.

We rang off.

It's an odd thing about talking to Rollo on the phone. Our mutual loathing doesn't transmit very well over copper wire. We talk like two normal people. I've never understood this, but I've never questioned it. I only know that when I'm in his physical presence I react the way Superman reacts to kryptonite—I try to get away as fast as I can. But Rollo is stuck in his cage and can't run anywhere. Of course when we're in each other's presence I am fully aware of this, and I do my best to help him by hurrying things along. Again, it's the WWI thing—a gentleman's war.

I'm sure that if our situations were reversed, Rollo would hasten to flee at the sight of me.

I gathered my accoutrement, then went to my *Lolita* and pulled out my starting cash. Okay. I'll admit it. I counted the dough twice. It's not that I don't trust the Denver Police Department, it's just that I always count my money after my secret hiding places have been groped by strangers.

I closed up shop and started down the fire escape. From that height I could see the spot farther along 13th where I had been pulled over by the police on Tuesday. I imagined that most of my neighbors could see it, too. I imagined that my neighbors had seen the cop cars that had filled the dirt lot like a demolition derby. I imagined that my neighbors were watching me climb down my fire escape at this very moment. If I had a neighbor like me, I would never take my eyes off me. In fact, I would wonder what I was doing on the fire escape when it was obvious that I ought to be in jail. Who is this guy from the top-floor apartment who gets visited all the time by the fuzz? I would probably get together with my neighbors and demand that I be evicted.

It was a few minutes before ten when I drove into the Rocky lot. In a way it felt sort of pleasant to be coming to work at ten instead of seven. If I had been able to do that at Dyna-Plex I would probably still be working there. I don't think big business understands employees at all. For one thing, most employees don't actually do anything while at work. I certainly was not an anomaly at Dyna-Plex. I very rarely ran into anybody at the office who did anything except drain the water cooler. Whenever the delivery man used to arrive with his big blue bottles of pure water, practically everybody in the office would come to watch him replace the empties with full bottles. I think the secretaries liked to look at the guy because he was young and muscular and wore sleeveless T-shirts. I think the junior executives liked to look at him because they had never seen anybody work before and it intrigued them.

I myself liked to watch him simply because I enjoy seeing other people do things I don't have to do.

Just before I opened the door to the on-call room, I took a deep breath and let it out slowly. It was time to face Rollo again. I suddenly felt like a vaudevillian who had been working the RKO circuit from Schenectady to Petaluma for fourteen years and was getting tired of performing the same old act. But—the show must go on. I wondered what Rollo would do if I entered the room on a unicycle.

I walked up to the cage and pulled out my billfold and removed three twenty-dollar bills. I tried to act casual as I slid the money toward him.

"Sixty dollars," he said, looking at my eyes. "Let's see. You're pulling a nine-hour shift, so you only owe me for three-fourths of a full shift. That would come to three-fourths of seventy dollars."

I held his gaze and swallowed hard.

"If I subtracted three-fourths of seventy dollars from sixty dollars, I wonder how much change I would owe you," Rollo said.

I tried to hold steady, but I was starting to sweat.

"Hmmmm?" he said.

I mentally tried to divide seventy by four and multiply the answer by three and subtract the total from sixty. Need I say more?

He had me on the ropes and he knew it.

I gritted my teeth.

"Making change is your job," I said. "I just drive."

That was as close as I ever came to saying "You win" to Rollo.

He smiled his infuriating Victor Buono smile and slowly counted out seven dollars and fifty cents.

I snatched up the money and shoved it into my jeans pocket, then I waited as he pretended to search around for my key and trip-sheet. He was relishing the moment.

I took the key and sheet and walked out of the on-call room filled with the kind of energy that only total humiliation can generate. I was ready to hit the road running. I checked 123 for dents and dings, stayed as far away from the radiator cap as humanly possible, and climbed into the driver's seat. I radioed the dispatcher and told him I was on the road.

"Did you bring a tardy slip?" he said.

"Up yours," I said.

"If you want an el-two, I can arrange it."

The Sunshine Boys were back on stage, but the act was getting old.

I started the engine and drove out of the lot. My instinct was to turn off the Rocky radio, turn on the AM, and forget I existed. After I gassed up and bought a Twinkie and soda, I had the urge to head over to the Brown Palace, but I needed to take radio calls that day. I was like a salmon that wanted badly to return to its spawning grounds, minus the horrendous ambition it took to climb a waterfall.

As I have said, there was no real problem with earning fifty dollars during a short-shift, it simply involved hard work. "Hard" is just a euphemism though. There is nothing hard about cab driving. "Steady" is the right word. But I'll stick with "hard" because to me, working steady is hard. When I pick up fares one right after another without a break, I always feel like I'm missing out on something. I feel like I need to take at least a half hour out of every hour just to observe my surroundings and get my bearings. On the rare day that I do work twelve hours without a single break, I come home feeling like I had just gotten out of the army and the old neighborhood had completely changed and all my pals had gotten married and moved to the suburbs. Working hard makes me feel lonely.

On the plus side, if I were to take one call right after another for twelve hours a day, I could afford to take two spring breaks a month. And if I drove five days a week like my friend Big Al and worked hard twelve hours a day, I would end up working one week a month and still give the IRS Xerox copies of my 1040 every year. But I'm the kind of person who cannot be tempted by money. Which is to say, if the PUC doubled the meter rates, I would work only half as many hours as I do now and still come out financially normal at the end of the month. All in all, I try to avoid plus sides.

I started taking calls. I made the proper attitude adjustment that an experienced asphalt warrior needs if he is to succeed at raking in the dough. I put out of my mind the fact that it was her word against mine. But every time I picked up a fare at an apartment building or outside a grocery store, the phrase kept popping into my head: "Her word against mine." It was a like a duel that I kept winning. It would pop in, and I would knock it right back out. I was like George Kennedy in *Cool Hand Luke* when he and Paul Newman had a boxing match in the "yard," and Newman wouldn't quit fighting. He kept coming back for more, and Kennedy kept knocking him to the ground, which got to be boring. The symbolism was so obvious that I went up to the theater snack-stand and bought a box of popcorn. A few years later I was watching *One Flew Over the Cuckoo's Nest* and I realized that it was the same story as *Cool Hand Luke*, i.e., an irrepressible free spirit comes into a place filled with incarcerated men who are being crushed by The System. He changes their lives and gives them hope—but in the end he's destroyed. Strother Martin was the best Big Nurse I ever saw.

CHAPTER 18

I jumped a bell at a Safeway store on east Colfax and drove the fare eight blocks. She had only one sack of groceries, so I didn't have the trauma of carrying dozens of white plastic bags into her house. That is the main reason I deliberately avoid working grocery stores. A cabbie can make fifteen to twenty dollars an hour if he focuses on grocery runs, but the problem—again—is that you have to work hard, or steady, or whatever you want to call it. But I wasn't being choosy that Wednesday. Drop off a fare and grab another bell, that was my approach.

Whenever I copped a fare that had more than one carry-on item, so to speak, I looked into the backseat afterward to make certain he or she hadn't left anything behind, such as a hundred thousand dollars. This was another of the many psychological tics that I had picked up in my years of cab driving, and I feared it would never stop ticking.

As soon as I dropped off the Safeway fare, I got a call in a nearby neighborhood. An elderly black woman wanted to go to a nearby bank. I suppressed my bank tic. She had two little boys with her. She told me she would be in the bank for only a few minutes to cash a check, and asked that I watch the boys while she was inside. This would be a round-trip. A five-dollar fare at best, which amounted to ten dollars in thirty minutes. I would gross two hundred and forty dollars a day if I did trips like that all the time. See? My brain will never stop playing games.

As soon as the woman and the two little boys climbed into my backseat, I heard one of the boys say, "Uh oooh." I looked around. He was grinning and pointing at a small pile of sugar on the seat that had apparently leaked out of the grocery sack of the fare that I had picked up at Safeway.

I shook my head with what I hoped would appear to be mock exasperation even though it was real exasperation. I hadn't noticed the sugar. It was small, about the size of a dime. I told the woman about the previous fare.

"I do believe that lady must have had a hole in her sack," the woman said with a frown.

The boys giggled. I told them not to touch it, that I would clean it up when we got to the bank.

After we got there I held the door open for the woman, then I opened my toolbox where I keep a variety of things too numerous to enumerate, but one of them was a small package of Kleenex. I proceeded to sweep the sugar out of the backseat. The boys helped me by brushing it with their fingers. "Thanks," I said. "I'll give each of you a quarter for helping me."

"I want a dollar!" the littlest boy said. I liked that. He was a straight-from-the-shoulder entrepreneur.

"Hush," his older brother said.

I gave them their quarters. The woman came out of the bank. I drove them home. The fare came to four dollars total, but I didn't mentally subtract the fifty cents that I had given to the kids. I placed the paying of the fifty cents into the same category that I place buying Twinkies. I never subtract "slush-fund" money that I spend on a given day.

But I started thinking about that pile of sugar. The fare that I had picked up at Safeway surely had noticed the sugar on the seat, but hadn't said anything to me about it. It was in a compact little pile, like a Hershey's Kiss. She was probably embarrassed. It didn't make me mad though. I understood. I've fled plenty of embarrassing situations. It's only human. Plus, I've policed up a lot more interesting things than sugar in my backseat, but that was in the days when I worked nights, when I was a newbie trying to figure out how to make the most money driving a cab. That was way before I figured out how to make the least money without starving to death. I picked up drunks from the bars at two a.m. back then. You find all sorts of things, both solids and liquids, when you work the bars.

Back then I had gotten into the habit of checking the backseat every time a drunk got out of my cab, or worse, jumped out of my cab without paying. After I gave up on nights and started driving days, I got out of the habit of checking the backseat. I decided I should start developing that habit again. But I didn't have much hope. I was like a guy who joins a gym and pays a two-hundred-and-fifty-dollar annual fee, and then goes there twice and lifts weights and never goes back again. But he did it because he thought that by spending a wad of dough he would feel guilty if he didn't make it to the gym three days a week. Little did he realize that he was one of those people who could not be motivated by money to do anything at all. He still gets letters in the mail offering to renew his membership "At Half Price!!!" There must be a lot of people like him in Denver.

I was headed west on Colfax, listening to the radio and trying to work my way over to The Hill, and in thinking about sugar and drunks I suddenly began to get an eerie feeling.

I was nearing Colorado Boulevard. I was not that far away from my crow's nest in terms of time or space. Maybe five minutes if I hit all the lights green. It was two-thirty in the afternoon and I had already grossed eighty-five dollars. Not a record by any means, but adequate. I made a left onto Colorado Boulevard and cruised up to 13th and turned right. I drove past the penny lady's house "her word against mine" and kept going. I was starting to sweat. I wanted to go to a "safe" place. Wichita was too far, so I drove to my apartment building, pulled into the dirt lot, and parked in the choice V-spot.

I sat for a moment staring at my rear-view mirror, then I climbed out of 123 and took a long look around the neighborhood to see if anybody was watching me. I couldn't tell. I didn't see the flicker of window shades.

I swallowed hard and climbed into the backseat, which still had a few bits of sugar granules scattered around. Try policing up sugar without a whisk broom. Good luck. I took one last glance through the windows, then knelt on the backseat and jammed my hand down into the space where the seat met the back, the space where I had found a plethora of combs, wallets, and a few empty pints. I felt something. I pulled it out and found myself staring at a stack of one-hundred dollar bills bound by a strip of paper stamped with the words "Glendale Bank & Trust."

Did this single stack of bills add up to one-hundred thousand dollars? I drew upon my knowledge of James Michener paperbacks. There was no way this stack of bills was the equivalent of a thousand pages. I guessed three hundred, tops. I tried to multiply three hundred times one hundred. I had never tried to carry so many zeros in my life. How do you multiply zeros by zeros fer the luvva Christ? I couldn't do it. So I went visual. I pictured a blackboard in my mind. I was old enough to have attended schools where the blackboards were actually black. Now they're green. Yeah. Sure. Now Johnny can read.

Sister Mary Denton was standing at the blackboard with a piece of chalk drawing zeros. I could see them. Three zero zero times one zero zero. Then she started placing zeros like a staircase under the line, or whatever it's called. The next thing I knew I was looking at 30,000. All I needed was a dollar sign on the left side and the picture was complete. I was holding thirty grand in my hand! Mr. Hollister had shoved it down behind the seat during the trip. But why?

I shoved my hand down behind the cushion and fished around, and touched another stack, and another, and another. I pulled them out. This gave me a total of four. I couldn't feel any others down there, but if this was all, then I was looking at something in the neighborhood of one-hundred thousand dollars.

I knelt in the backseat staring at the money and thinking that I had been driving around since Monday afternoon with a tenth of a million dollars at my back. It made my scalp prickle. I felt as if I was staring at something real for the first time in my life. Those four neatly trimmed compact blocks of green brick seemed to throb with a life of their own, which they did, because they were real. They weren't just paper. They were all the things that a hundred thousand dollars could buy, not counting a house. You might be able to buy half a house with that nowadays, but there was once a time when you could have bought five or six houses, depending on location and contemporary market trends.

"I should call the police."

I said this out loud to make it real, because the thought wasn't real enough. Thoughts are as silent as smoke. They're less real than words, which are mere sounds. Talk is cheap and thoughts are cheaper, like thinking about writing a novel and telling your friends the plot but never getting around to writing it, yet pretending that your book is real because you made it as far as sound waves that can be heard, rather than ink that can be smelled.

"I should call the police right away."

I reached into the front seat and picked up my plastic briefcase and put it in the backseat and shoved the stacks inside it. I closed the briefcase as tight as it would go, then grabbed it by the handle and backed out of the cab and shut the door.

I closed the driver's door and walked across the dirt lot. There were no other cars in the lot. All the other tenants were at work or wherever they went in the daytime. I didn't know because I had never met any of my neighbors, had never spoken to any of them, and had no interest in asking them where they worked out of fear they would interpret it as an invitation to give me even more uninteresting details about their lives.

I climbed the fire escape and unlocked the door to my crow's nest and entered the kitchen, set the briefcase on the table, and walked into the living room where my telephone was waiting for me. I sat down on my easy chair and looked at the phone.

"Maybe I should call the hospital. Ottman and Quigg are probably there. I should try that first, and if they're not there, I'll call DPD."

I got up and walked into the kitchen and grabbed the briefcase and carried it back to my easy chair and sat down.

I opened the briefcase and pulled out a stack and looked at the bills. The portrait on the top bill was hidden under the wrapper, but I knew who was hiding under there: Ben Franklin, my favorite colonist. He invented bifocals and the rocking chair.

"If I can't get hold of Ottman and Quigg, maybe I should ask for Duncan and Argyle." It probably wouldn't come as a surprise to them to hear that I had found one-hundred thousand dollars in my taxi, and would they please come over and pick it up. Nothing I did would surprise Duncan and Argyle. They would probably be glad to hear from me for once.

Except the operator would probably put me right through to Ottman and Quigg, or radio a quick message. They would call me right back. Mere minutes. They would send a black-and-white over right away. Capitol Hill is a small beat. Cops everywhere.

I started riffling a stack the way a gambler riffles a deck of cards before dealing stud. I slowed my riffle and tried to count the number of bills. One two three four … but my hands were trembling a bit.

I felt funny inside.

I felt like I had swallowed a quick cup of joe and wasn't handling the infusion of caffeine very well. I know how that feels because I sometimes do it on purpose, a quick cup at a 7-11 while shooting the bull with an ex-Rocky driver, then buying another cup for the road. That's one of the benefits of giving up cab driving and going to work at a kwickie-mart: joe on tap. Tempting. Be like working in a bar. I'd make a terrible bartender. Short-lived career at best. Liquor bottles stacked in front of a mirror. Tempting. Darn that temptation anyway. Like quick infusions of hot caffeine. Makes the world spin.

My head felt light. I stopped riffling the money and set it on my lap. I seemed to have put the briefcase on the table after taking the money out. In fact I had put it on top of the telephone. I had a lap full of money.

"I should call right now."

I reached for the briefcase and accidentally knocked the phone to the floor. Awkward business, trying to do things with a cluttered lap.

I gathered up the money and set it on the table and stood up and bent over and picked up the phone and placed it on the table next to the money.

"There."

I sat back down. Time to make the call. Get the cops over here right away. Maybe they'll send the S.W.A.T team.

I started thinking about this morning's roust. What if I had been asleep? What if they had busted the door down? That would have been a shock, waking up to cops storming in. But that's how they like to do it, isn't it? Catch the culprit unawares. Best strategy.

Searched my apartment high and low. Didn't find a thing. Clean slate. Tabula rasa. Except for my steamer trunk of broken dreams. A hundred manuscripts I had told them. But were there really that many? Maybe more. Lost count years ago. Christ, how many years have I been writing novels? How many years have I been trying to make a big score off the publishing world? Dropped out of WSU and told Mary Margaret Flaherty that I was leaving town and going out into the world to become a writer. Make a million. Or at least a hundred thousand.

Cops didn't find anything. The bust was a wash. Duncan and Argyle could have assured them. Murph the taxi driver? Innocent as a newborn babe. Gets himself into the craziest fixes, but always comes out smelling like a rose because he hasn't got a corrupt bone in his body. Don't even bother with a search warrant. Just ask him if he stole the money. He won't lie. He never lies to cops. He's a treat.

Searched my place from top to bottom.

Came up empty-handed.

False trail.

Clean slate.

Mr. Hollister in the cardiac unit at DGH on the verge of death. If he died, that would be that. Money never found. Insurance pays off the bank. Case kept open by the police until it's buried under so much dust that nobody can read the witness statements. Shunted to the rear by newer crimes and criminals. A lot of cases go unsolved.

"If Mr. Trowbridge had left something hidden in your taxi, would it have been obliterated by the fire?"

What's that?

A fragment of a conversation that took place a long time ago. It drifted into my mind as I stared at the telephone. I had a cab burn up on me one time. Made the police a bit suspicious. Duncan and Argyle on that case. Missing person. Possible suicide. Possible robbery. Possible murder. Anything is possible in the crazy world of cab driving. Funny that I would recall it now. I try not to recall everything.

But I was feeling funny that afternoon. The money lay heavy on my lap. Somehow it had gotten back there. I didn't remember picking it up. It reminded me of my trip home at Christmas. A niece had sat on my lap while I was watching football hi-lites with my drunk uncles. Couldn't have weighed more than thirty pounds, but these four stacks of bills weighed a lot more than Betsy. One of Shannon Lucy's kids. Sister of Steven, my computer-nerd nephew. Knew all about operating the RamBlaster 4000 that my brother Gavin had given me in lieu of the traditional box of typewriter ribbons. "I only know that Tommy Malloy got a three-book deal from Scribner's after he bought a computer," Gavin had said. He wanted to see me succeed at writing and decided a word processor was the key to making The Big Money, and I was short on keys right then. That's how he defined literary success. Money. Could read me like an X-ray.

I looked at the computer resting in the corner of my living room. A bit dusty. I used to store my Smith-Corona on the top shelf of my closet when I wasn't using it to write novels, but the RamBlaster was too big to lug around. I was forced to look at it when I was "in between" novels. Maybe I should have left the computer in the bedroom. But then I would have been forced to look at my steamer trunk containing all my unsold novels. How many novels? How many years?

What if—hypothetically speaking—my cab somehow burned up today? I mean the cab down in the parking lot, Rocky Mountain Taxicab #123, the vehicle I had been given as a replacement for #127, which had burned up near the viaducts.

"If Mr. Trowbridge had left something hidden in your taxi, would it have been obliterated by the fire?"

"You better believe it!" I chirped. "There was nothing left of that cab but a charcoal briquette!"

Just for the sake of argument, let's say that somehow #123 burned to a crisp. Two cabs in one year. Would that seem like a coincidence? But then Hogan had told them that it happens every once in awhile. Old heaps. Former police interceptors turned into vehicles of urban transportation with a couple hundred thousand miles already racked up on the odometer by Denver's finest. Air conditioner overtaxed and the next thing I knew the Denver Fire Department was roaming around in their yellow space-suits ignoring the flames. Bang bang bang bang went the tires. Thought I was going to get arrested for reckless parking, littering, something, but the cop just drove away, and the firefighters drove away, and the tow truck drove away with the husk of me ol' pal #127, and it was as if nothing had happened and nobody cared. Not even Duncan and Argyle.

A dry radiator would certainly be a good explanation. How many miles had I driven from Chambers and Arapahoe without a drop of water in the cooling system? Might have caused a bit of internal damage that the mechanics in the garage had overlooked. The whole show could go up in flames. Happens all the time, according to Hogan.

"You must harbor a secret in your past so dreadful and shameful that the mere thought of it sends you lurching violently to the nearest liquor store."

What's that?

A fragment of a conversation that took place a long time ago.

No—I read it somewhere. Yes. It was printed on a five-dollar bill. Trowbridge. The man I was suspected of murdering. Related indirectly to the cab-burning business. Had nothing to do with it though. Mere coincidence. Duncan and Argyle couldn't forge a link. Dismissed as irrelevant.

The police raid my apartment and find nothing, then 123 burns up, and then Mr. Hollister expires without regaining consciousness. Just for the sake of argument, what would be the implications of three such unlikely coincidences? Let's see. Failed search warrant, combined with the sheer impossibility of sifting through the ruins of a vehicle of public transportation reduced to a briquette—plus, no living witness.

Scot-free.

Clean slate.

My brain felt funny.

I don't know how long I sat there alone in my crow's nest with the stacks of money clutched to my breast. I was unaware of the passage of time. I was unaware of the silence. I was gazing toward the far wall above my TV set, my eyes focused at a random point halfway between my face and the wall, a distance of perhaps seven feet. Which is to say, I wasn't looking at anything at all. Not outside of my head anyway. I was looking at images inside my head. They made me feel funny. They made me feel like I was drinking thick, black, strong coffee.

Then the phone rang.

I was startled out of my reverie.

I was sitting so close to the phone that my left shoulder jerked as if a snake had struck it.

The phone rang a second time.

I rubbed my shoulder. It hurt. But this helped to keep me in touch with reality. My answering machine always rings five times, giving the caller five chances to hang up in disgust. Right then I wished I owned a machine that offered ten chances to give up, but into each life a little rain must fall.

Before the recorded message started though, I reached over and touched a button that turned off the auto-answer. The phone continued to ring for a while, then it stopped. That felt good. It reminded me of the days when I didn't have an answering machine, when people got disgusted and never called back.

I looked down at the stacks of money.

I swallowed hard.

What had I been thinking?

Had I been thinking that I could successfully steal one-hundred thousand dollars?

Me?

Then I realized what was happening. I was experiencing my very first dark night of the soul. And here it was only three in the afternoon. According to F. Scott Fitzgerald, the dark night of the soul normally takes place at three o'clock in the morning. But knowing Fitzgerald, he was probably speaking metaphorically. Anybody who drank as much alcohol as he did could probably have a dark night of the soul while eating lunch at the Stork Club.

CHAPTER 19

I got up from my easy chair and stuffed the money back into my briefcase. My head still felt funny, but in a different way. I looked at the phone and decided that the thing to do would be to drive down to DPD and turn the money over to the police in person. That maneuver always seems to impress district attorneys. Jail time reduced from five to three. The results aren't immediate, but I imagine that when year #3 falls off the calendar, it makes a difference.

I carried the briefcase into the kitchen and opened the refrigerator and stood there staring at the fairly empty shelves. I forgot what I had opened the door for. Not a beer certainly. Imagine getting caught driving a taxi with alcohol in my system while hauling a hundred grand in stolen money. What district attorney would cut me a plea then? But I was busy thinking. Not a good thing to do when cold air is spilling out of the fridge. Nevertheless I stood there staring at a bottle of catsup and wondering why Mr. Hollister had stuffed the money down behind the backseat.

Unless …

Unless hiding the money in the rear of a taxi had been part of a scheme to orchestrate a getaway so perfect that not even Sam Peckinpah could have …

I stopped thinking.

I closed the door.

Then I remembered.

I opened the door and grabbed a soda and shut the door. I went to a kitchen window and lifted the curtain and peeked out.

What if somebody else knew that the money was in my backseat? What if somebody was out there right now, shadowing me in a car and watching my every move? Maybe Mr. Hollister had hidden the money so that a cohort could … say … call a taxi … a specific taxi … and make the pickup without my even knowing that the fare was digging around in the backseat. A perfect crime worthy of … me?

I asked myself how I could have entertained for even one second the idea that I might be able to maneuver my way through a series of illegal obstacles and get away scot-free with the money. This was what made my head feel funny. Prior to this it was the sight, the feel, the smell of the money in my possession that made me feel as if I was buzzed on caffeine. It was the same feeling I got on the day I started writing my first novel, convinced that I would get rich. It was a feeling unalloyed with doubt, and that's exactly how I had felt when I sat in my easy chair pretending I was going to call the police. I could draw only one conclusion: I was not as innocent as a newborn babe after all. I had never been that innocent, not even as a newborn babe.

I sensed that somewhere inside my body was a corrupt bone.

Oh it was in me all right.

It was there.

And it made me feel funny.

It didn't matter that I had overcome the temptation. First you have to feel the temptation before you can overcome it. Maybe you reject it right away. But then again … maybe you don't. But a person who didn't have any corrupt bones would reject it right off the bat. For instance, if a scalper offered me a primo ticket to a Bronco game, without thinking twice I would walk away. I'm never tempted to participate in spectator sports. When it comes to sitting on a cold bleacher in the winter, my bones are as pure as the driven snow.

On the other hand, if you have to wrestle with a decision whether or not to succumb to temptation, you're just kidding yourself. You are already corrupt, baby—I'm talking bad-to-the-bone. The source of your wrestling match is nothing more than a fear of getting caught. You've already made your decision. You want that thing so much, whatever it is, that you would do anything to get your hands on it—as long as you don't get caught.

These were the thoughts I had as I peeked through the curtain.

Yep.

I was bad-to-the-bone.

And for some reason I didn't like it.

A personality flaw like that could get me a nickel in Cañon City. And consider this—what if I had actually needed the hundred thousand? Say for instance the mob had its hooks in me and I needed to pay off a loan shark. Little things like that can tip the balance against you. Think how awful it would be to wake up every day in jail just because you overestimated your ability to tighten a radiator cap.

I let the curtain drop and stood contemplating the fact that I was the only person I knew whom I couldn't trust.

What if I handed the money over to Ottman and Quigg, and instead of saying, "Hey great, you found the money!" they said, "Well, well, you brought the money back, eh? My, my, isn't that interesting? But could it possibly be that you felt the noose tightening a little bit? Did that search warrant give you second thoughts, Murph? Maybe you figured you had better make it look like you oh-so-accidentally just happened to find the missing hundred-thousand and thought you could just waltz in here and hand it over to us and brush off your hands and walk away as innocent as a newborn babe, eh? Is that what you were thinking, Mister Murphy?"

I swallowed hard.

I was staring at nothing again. But I wasn't having a dark night of the soul. It was worse than that. I was thinking about the whimsical nature of innocence. Whose mind wouldn't be "turned" by the sight of a tenth-of-a-million dollars? Men had been known to ride Conestoga wagons all the way to California just to jump claims at Sutter's Mill. What—besides my massive ego—made me think I was different from anybody else? Sure, I always suspected that my ego was bigger than the average person's, but why would I assume that I was otherwise normal?

Jaysus.

The very presence of this money was acting upon my mind the way red kryptonite affects Superman. Green kryptonite of course can kill Superman, but red kryptonite merely has weird effects on him. For instance, in one comic book I read, Superman grew four extra arms after being exposed to red kryptonite. Clark Kent went through nine kinds of hell trying to hide his six arms from Lois Lane.

The point I'm trying to make is that the discovery of the money in my backseat was having an effect on me that I never would have believed. I mean, the most money I ever had in one stack was two thousand dollars, which I had brought home from the army. I didn't steal it though. They gave it to me. It was my separation pay, plus money I had saved up because I never bought anything. Not owning stuff was a practice I started in the army. If you owned stuff, you had to carry it yourself from one duty station to another. They didn't provide military butlers or anything. I got shipped to a lot of different duty stations for some reason, so my motto back then was: If it doesn't fit in my duffel bag, it doesn't fit in my life.

Suddenly I wanted out.

I wanted to turn the clock back an hour and make all of this not happen. I wanted to not know where the money was. I wanted to not know the secret of my bones. I wanted to be driving west on Colfax Avenue and listening to calls on the radio and not be thinking about spilled sugar or deadbeat drunks or anything other than making my profit for the day, then going home and trying not to think about the fact that it was "her word against mine."

I opened the door and stepped out onto the fire escape. I closed the door, which locked shut with a snap. I looked around the neighborhood wondering if someone was sitting on the front seat of a parked car along 13th Avenue watching my every move.

"Watch this, pal," I said out loud.

I was three stories up so it was unlikely that anyone heard me except maybe the tenant directly below my apartment, but he was probably at work. A woman once lived in that apartment. She used to sunbathe top-less on the second-floor landing of the fire escape, but let's move on.

I climbed down the metal staircase and crossed the parking lot to my cab. Without even pretending to be doing something other than what I was actually doing, which is rare for me, I opened the right-rear door and climbed in and sat down and opened my briefcase. I reached in and pulled out the four stacks and began stuffing them down behind the seat as I imagined Mr. Hollister had done on the short trip from the bank. I didn't know why Mr. Hollister had done it, but I sure as hell knew why I was doing it.

I climbed out of the cab and looked at the seat. Not a sign of tam-pering. As far as my backseat was concerned, it might as well have been one hour ago instead of now. I closed the door and walked around to the driver's side without bothering to see whether anyone was watching me. Again, this was rare. Whenever I drive to, for instance, the laundromat I glance surreptitiously around before I get into my Chevy. If anyone hap-pens to be watching me on those occasions, they just might get the im-pression that I am doing something important, which is exactly the way I want it. People who do laundry rarely get the opportunity to feel "special."

I started 123, backed around, and drove out to 13th. I turned right at the corner and drove down to 14th and headed toward Colorado Bou-levard. I kept the Rocky radio off. As far as I was concerned, I was putting Time itself on hold. I crossed Colorado, then made the circuit around the block and onto Colfax Avenue. I aimed the hood ornament west.

Everything was back to the way it had been before I had experienced that "eerie" feeling. I even drove past a telephone pole that I had been passing when the "eerie" feeling came over me. I knew that pole. I knew it well. Local bands used the pole to advertise gigs at nightclubs. It was right next to a bus stop. It was a good place to advertise. The telephone pole was plastered with tattered, weather-worn flyers. It looked cool, and sort of European. You don't see very much cool stuff in Denver.

I glanced at my wristwatch. Yes. Exactly one hour had passed since the advent of the "eerie" feeling. By "exactly" I mean "more-or-less." I reached down and turned on the Rocky radio. In doing so, I turned Time itself on again. The past hour had never happened. It was three-thirty now and not two-thirty but that couldn't be helped. Admittedly it was the kind of tiny detail that normally would have irritated me like a sticker burr in a sock, but I dealt with it by simply pretending that I had gone on Daylight Savings Time. I pretended that I had, in effect, moved America back one hour.

Or was it forward one hour?

This was late March, and the Mountain Time Zone had already switched, but I couldn't remember whether it was "spring forward and fall back," or "fall forward and spring back." Fall forward sounded right because of the repetition of the letter "F." On the other hand, I seemed to remember being irritated by the fact that there was no repetition of the letter "F" in that old saying, which was supposed to help people remember how to set their clocks. But most Coloradans rely on disk jockeys to set their clocks twice a year. It's hell living under socialism.

I drove west on Colfax, pleased with what I had done, and only slightly irritated by the fact that I wasn't precisely certain what I was supposed to be pretending, beyond the fact that I had moved somewhere in time by one hour. As far as I was concerned though, I was totally oblivious to the money stuffed down behind the backseat of my cab. Completely unaware of its existence. Utterly clueless. I was just an ordinary Joe trying to earn his daily bread before signing out at seven p.m.

I had already grossed eighty-five dollars, which put me a whole five dollars up for the day, but this didn't worry me. I had three-and-a-half hours left to gross forty-five bucks, and there was one thing I knew for certain: any cab driver who couldn't earn forty-five bucks in three-and-half hours needed some kind of goddamn therapy.

As I drove along oblivious to the money in my backseat I began to think about what might happen if my cab broke down and had to go into the shop for major repairs. At some point the mechanics might be required to remove the backseat, and one of them would find the stacks of money. His hat would probably bounce off the ceiling, especially if he was alone. If he was with somebody, both their hats would bounce off the ceiling. But after the hats were back on their heads, what would happen? Would they take the money to the foreman and say, "Look what we found"? Or would they glance at each other with the "knowing" look of co-conspirators and subsequently embark upon a journey that would lead to corruption, greed, and madness? I mean, if one-hundred thousand dollars made me feel funny, imagine what it would do to a mechanic.

But maybe they would take the money to Hogan. Maybe Hogan would put two-and-two together and realize that it was the money from the Glendale heist that had never been solved. By that time I might not be working at Rocky Cab anymore. Maybe I would be living in a bungalow in Southern California in the general vicinity of Beverly Hills, writing the screenplay version of my latest novel and sipping daiquiris by the swimming pool while young aspiring actresses did multiple laps in the water and then climbed out and swung their wet heads freely so that the excess moisture in their blonde hair would be whipped free from each delicate golden follicle. That could happen. Hogan would subsequently realize that the cloud of suspicion under which I had left had been lifted. He would call Ottman and Quigg and tell them the money had been found behind the backseat, and they would all have a good laugh.

But ... what if Ottman and Quigg and Hogan and the mechanics realized that nobody else knew about the money? Imagine what an amount of money like that could do to the heads of two underpaid cops, a taxi supervisor, and two auto mechanics. It could end up like a remade low-budget cable-TV version of *The Treasure of the Sierra Madre*.

I suddenly realized that by simply leaving the money under the back-seat and doing absolutely nothing at all, I could destroy the lives of five good men.

CHAPTER 20

I had never suspected that knowledge could have so many drawbacks.
The fact that the money was lying under the backseat made it impossible for me to think about anything else. I felt like I had planted a time
bomb that could damage other people even though "technically" I wasn't
the one who had put the money there. Mr. Hollister had done it, although I still didn't know why. And I didn't want to know. But as I drove
west on Colfax that day I knew I was lying to myself. I, in fact, did want
to know. For one thing, I wanted to know if there was a co-conspirator
following me and waiting for an opportune moment to dry-gulch me
with a sap. That's the kind of thing you can't get out of your mind even
if you somehow manage to stop thinking about one-hundred thousand
dollars for five seconds. Was I being followed?

What if he had seen me jam the money down under the seat, and
knew he had to strike while the iron was hot. Leap at the chance. Seize
the moment. Grab the bull. Bird in the hand. He who hesitates. For all
I knew he was driving the gray Ford that had been tailgating me for the
past two blocks. He had seen me replace the money where I had found
it, and now he was trying to read my mind, psyche out my motive, an-
ticipate my next move. He had played this game before, whereas I was
just a cabbie, a nobody, an amateur playing a game with rules I didn't
understand.

My corpse might turn up in the Platte.

It's a funny thing about Denver—you never read stories in the paper
about bodies turning up in the Platte River, or even in Cherry Creek. Of

course they're pretty shallow rivers. Compared to the Mississippi they're not even rivers at all—they're mere trickles compared to The Ol' Man. Of course we do have the Rocky Mountains, which makes up for our sissy rivers. But it's a funny thing about the Rocky Mountains. They seem to be associated primarily with Colorado, even though they run from Canada clear down through New Mexico. I've always wondered if this annoys the people of Wyoming. I guess we Coloradans just got lucky. Not that I'm really a Coloradan. I was born in Kansas. But I guess if you live somewhere long enough, you become a part of The Big Lie.

I turned left onto Broadway. I knew where I was going. I had known it the moment I walked out the door. I had known it when I was stuffing the money down in the backseat. I had known it when I was idly daydreaming about Wyoming where I buy my firecrackers every Fourth of July because Colorado won't sell them to me or anybody else. I was headed for Denver General Hospital.

I pulled into the parking lot across the street and paid a buck and headed for the DGH doors. I entered, walked to an elevator, and got on. I knew the route. I had been there before. I sometimes have dreams that I'm wandering around the corridors of a hospital looking for a restroom. One time I dreamed I walked into a restroom and the toilet was at the very top of a tower of porcelain that reminded me of the Matterhorn ride in Disneyland. If I ever go to a psychiatrist, I plan to mention this.

The elevator door opened and I stepped out into a large waiting room where people were seated on plastic chairs. Who was the genius that named the waiting room? I turned to my left and headed for the corridor that would lead me to the cardiac unit. Maybe Ottman and Quigg would be there, but if not, I figured I could ask one of the guards to whisper into his shoulder and ask HQ to send the detectives over to speak with their prime suspect, i.e., me.

I turned right and walked to the end of the hall, then left again. Then I stopped. I seemed to have taken a wrong turn somewhere. I backtracked, but I didn't recognize what would have been my return route from the last time I was at the hospital, assuming I was in the correct corridor. I decided not to assume. Then it occurred to me that the last time I was here Quigg and I had come out of a bank of elevators on the far side of the waiting room, which meant I should originally have turned to my right.

But I continued to walk down the hallway. I was too embarrassed to turn around and walk back. Whenever I passed a nurse or a man pushing a dust mop, I adjusted my facial expression to look as if I knew exactly where I was going. I was forced to improvise because I had never looked that way before.

After five minutes of wandering around the building I suddenly found myself back in the waiting room. I walked to the middle of the floor and looked around, then noticed that there were signs with big red arrows indicating the various medical wards. I felt that everyone in the waiting room was watching me, so I tried to adjust my facial expression so that I looked like I was merely examining the signs in order to confirm what I already knew. This played hell with my facial muscles but I think I pulled it off. Here's the funny part though—I realized I had originally walked down the correct corridor after all.

Once again I walked down the hall, trying to picture in my mind the doorway to the room that I was looking for in the way that Tony Perkins pretended to make a mental picturization of Janet Leigh while Martin Balsam pretended to believe his phony story—the difference being that I was actually picturizing.

It didn't work. I couldn't find the room. I finally swallowed my pride and went up to the nurse's desk and asked how to get to Mr. Hollister's room.

"Are you a member of the family?" she said.

"No, I'm just a suspect."

"I'm sorry," she said, "but Mr. Hollister passed away two hours ago."

I blinked once, then almost said, "When will he be back?"

But I understood what she meant. It just took a few seconds to sink in. I wasn't used to news like that. But after it sank, I didn't know what to say. I just stared at the nurse, and she stared at me. For some reason I suddenly felt the need to justify my existence, so I said, "I'm a taxi driver."

She raised her eyebrows. "Oh? Did somebody from this floor call a taxi?"

"I don't know," I said. "Thank you for …"

That's as far as I got before I turned and walked away. It seemed like I walked for an awful long time. After awhile I started looking for a restroom. It gave me an "eerie" feeling but I stuck with it. Sometimes in my dreams I walk into a restroom that is as small as a phone booth and the urinal is at eye-level. If I ever get any goddamn therapy, that shrink's gonna get his money's worth.

After using a seemingly normal restroom, I found my way out of the hospital and walked across the street to the parking lot. My cab was still there. I looked in the window. The backseat was still there. Through the use of inductive logic I chose to believe that the money was still there. I climbed into the driver's seat and sat staring out the front window thinking about poor ol' Willy Loman. Pulled a bank job, then died of heart attack.

Then I realized that of the three elements of the perfect crime that I had visualized during my dark night of the soul, two of them had come to pass: a fruitless search warrant, and a dead robbery suspect. All I had to do now was set fire to my taxi, and it was hello Tahiti.

The windows were rolled up and the hot sun was streaming through the windshield. It was as warm as I imagined Gilligan's island must be. The real island, not the TV island. By "real" I mean an island in the South Pacific where a writer could lie in a hammock all day long and think about the plot of his next novel. If he was rich enough, he could hire a Mary Ann look-alike to mix rum drinks and wait on him hand-and-foot. But there wouldn't be any hanky-panky. Nosir. He would be a man of such impeccable integrity that the mere thought of dallying with Mary Ann would grievously offend his moral sensibilities. He would be the exact opposite of me.

I don't know how long I sat in the taxi, but by the time I twisted the ignition I had come to a couple of conclusions. Number one: I was the walking embodiment of pure evil. Number two: I had to return the money.

I drove down to 6th Avenue and headed east. I could have taken a shorter route but I wanted to avoid side streets and stop signs. I intended to hit all the green lights up Lincoln and swing over to DPD. I turned on the radio.

"One twenty-three. El-two."

That figured.

I picked up the mike.

"Check."

I hung up the mike.

I turned off the radio. I looked at my wristwatch. It was four-thirty. I had grossed five dollars for the day and I had two-and-a-half hours left on my shift. I thought back over the past couple of days and realized that I had earned a minus twenty dollars for the week. This was so off-the-charts ludicrous that I would have laughed except I was thinking about poor ol' Willy Loman. "Worth more dead than alive," according to Arthur Miller. I wondered if Arthur Miller had coined that phrase, or if it was a common phrase back in the old days. Or maybe he had heard some guy say it once and filed it away for future use after he became a playwright. Then I wondered if the guy subsequently said, "Hey, that's my phrase!" and tried to sue Miller for plagiarism. Non-writers place a much greater value on sentences than editors do.

Even though I was hauling around one-hundred thousand dollars, the fact that this week was financially shot to pieces didn't really bother me. I already knew what I was going to do. I was going to pretend that this was my spring break week, and just drive for the next three weeks until my financial status was copacetic again. You never win and you never lose in the cab game. It's all in the mind. That's both the bad news and the best news you'll ever hear.

I continued along 6th until I got to University, then I turned north and took the long straight route to Rocky Cab. When I arrived I pulled into an empty space near the door to the on-call room. I grabbed my accoutrement and got out, entered the room and walked past Rollo without looking at him. I climbed the stairs to Hogan's office and almost shoved the door open without knocking. I had gone through this so many times that it seemed choreographed, that Hogan was the director of a tragedy in which I was the star, that he wouldn't even expect me to knock. But beyond that, I had been there so often that I felt I had graduated to the status of a "special" person to whom the rules did not apply. Of course, waking up in the morning also gave me that feeling.

"Yeah," Hogan said, after I discreetly knocked.

I shoved the door open and saw Ottman and Quigg peering at me. It was like looking at a photograph with the faces of Duncan and Argyle airbrushed in. My life was a broken record in a room full of faded photographs. I didn't even go through the boring ritual of sitting down in my chair before I said, "I know where the money is that was stolen from the bank."

"You do?" Ottman and Quigg said simultaneously.

I nodded. Then I walked across the room and sat down on my chair. I crossed my legs and looked up at the detectives.

This room was mine.

I owned it.

The three men stared at me, and for the first time in my life I didn't relish being the center of attention. You oughta see me when I do relish it—I'm the life of the party.

"It's under the backseat of my taxi," I said. "I found it stuffed down behind the cushion."

Ottman and Quigg glanced at each other.

There was a moment of silence. Then Ottman moved around in front of me. Quigg surreptitiously took his place between myself and the only escape route from the room.

"What motivated you to look under the seat cushion?" Ottman said.

"Fourteen years of adding artifacts to my comb collection," I said.

"Come again?"

"I've never been very good at arithmetic, Detective Ottman, but today for the first time in my life I added two-plus-two and I got four."

"The seat cushion, Murph. What made you look under the seat cushion?"

"Logic. I don't know whether it was deductive or inductive logic. Maybe a little of both. You be the judge. But after you told me the briefcase was empty I started trying to put two-and-two together. I had an edge over you because I knew for a fact that I hadn't taken the money out of the briefcase. I knew you weren't going to find the money when you searched my apartment, but there was no point in telling you that. I know how the game is played. I watch a lot of cop shows. So I kept my mouth shut. And I waited. And when you came up empty-handed I wasn't surprised. I'm never surprised when people come to me for money and walk away empty-handed.

"Originally I thought maybe Mr. Hollister got mugged after he climbed out of my taxi that afternoon. Maybe he had the misfortune of running into someone just like himself. Only younger. And stronger. Maybe there was a struggle in the parking lot and he lost. Maybe it was fate that he just happened to run into a mugger. But the problem was, I've never had much faith in fate. It's too convenient. Bad luck I can understand. But fate? Save it for the late show."

"The seat cushion, Murph. Why did you look under the seat cushion?"

I nodded at Ottman. It was a nod that said, Try this on for size.

"When I first started driving a taxi fourteen years ago, they advised us to look into the backseat every time a fare climbed out because fares sometimes leave things behind. Briefcases. Billfolds. Cameras. Books. Combs. You name it. If a human being can leave it behind, I've picked it up, swept it out, or sponged it off. But I got out of the habit because it didn't happen often enough to give me the psychological tic that an asphalt … that a cab driver needs to keep on doing the right thing. But maybe that's because we're only human. We're as lazy as the next guy. We wouldn't be human if we weren't lazy. But this afternoon around two o'clock I decided to stop being human and start being responsible. I decided I would start looking into the backseat every time someone got out of my cab."

I paused a moment, but nobody said anything. I continued.

"As soon as I decided that, I started to get an eerie feeling. I've found a lot of things that have fallen between the crack of the cushions in the rear. Combs and books and cameras and billfolds. I even found a string of lovebeads one time, but that was long ago, and in another mess. Then it hit me. Mr. Hollister could have left the money in my cab, and there was only one place I knew of where he could have put it. That's when I pulled over to take a look. Just a look. I didn't know for sure. I've never known anything for sure. I was placing my faith in logic. But like I said, it might have been inductive logic because I had found lots of things down there before and might find one more thing. Or deductive—because I had found a lot of things down there and might find one more. You tell me. All I know is, I stuck my hand down the crack of my backseat and pulled out a stack of bills bound with a wrapper stamped by the Glendale Bank & Trust."

"Do you have it with you?"

"I put it back where I found it."

Glance.

"Is it in your taxi right now?"

"Yes."

"Show us," Ottman said.

CHAPTER 21

The four of us walked down the stairwell. We didn't attract any attention as we walked out of the on-call room. My cab was parked right by the door. I pointed at it. "Do you want me to do the honors?" I said.

But Quigg stepped forward and opened the right-rear door.

"The stacks of money are near the middle," I said. "He must have stuffed them down there with his left hand."

Quigg knelt on the backseat and slipped his hand down the crack and felt around. A moment later he pulled out a stack of dough.

"There's three more down there," I said.

Quigg backed out of the car and handed the money to Ottman. They examined the wrapper, then Quigg looked at me. "Can that seat be removed?"

Hogan and I teamed up to do the honors. I walked around to the left-rear door and opened it, and together Hogan and I grabbed the seat by the slats and worked it away from the back cushion. And there, among a collection of greasy dust, chewing gum, and combs, lay three more stacks of hundred-dollar bills.

Ottman leaned into the rear and looked closely at them, then got back out. He asked Hogan to bring him a manila envelope. Hogan went into the on-call room, and came out a few moments later. Ottman picked up the stacks from the floor and placed them into the envelope.

"I'll need you to lock up your taxi, Murph," Ottman said. "You won't be driving it any more today. Leave everything just the way it is. I'm going to call headquarters and have some people come down here."

I made sure all the windows were rolled tight, then I locked the doors. The four of us went back inside and walked up to Hogan's office.

I sat on my chair while Ottman made a phone call to his superiors. After he hung up, he turned to me and said, "I have something important to tell you, Murph."

I looked up at him. "Does it have anything to do with the fact that Mr. Hollister is dead?"

Ottman glanced at Quigg.

Then he nodded.

"That's one of the reasons we came here this afternoon, Murph. I asked Mr. Hogan to call you in because I wanted to clarify for you the status of the case." Ottman pulled "his" chair over and sat down facing me. "Mr. Hollister died three hours ago. But before he died, he regained consciousness long enough to tell our man what he had done."

"You mean long enough to confess?" I said.

Ottman nodded.

He glanced at the floor. "My partner and I were not at the hospital, but one of the guards gave us a call and told us that Mr. Hollister was awake and wanted to talk. However by the time we got there, he was dead. He did talk though. He told the uniformed guard everything. Mr. Hollister confessed that he had stuffed the money down behind the backseat of the taxi that he had ridden in on the day he robbed the Glendale Bank & Trust."

I stared at Ottman for a few moments, digesting what he had just said. Then I spoke.

"So you already knew."

"Yes. Mr. Hollister died twenty minutes before my partner and I arrived at DGH. We took a report from the guard, and then we came here and asked Mr. Hogan to call you in."

"But why?" I said.

"Why what?"

"Why did Mr. Hollister stuff the money down behind the backseat?"

"Because he panicked."

That caught my attention. I know all about panic. I knew so much about panic that I had learned to live with it, to work around it, and especially to avoid it, the same way the one-armed man learned to avoid David Janssen. If you don't know who David Janssen was, don't panic. It doesn't matter. But I wanted to tell Detective Ottman that it seemed to me that Mr. Hollister had picked the wrong time to panic. I myself would have panicked the moment I started thinking about robbing a bank.

Or would I?

"You see, Murph, Mr. Hollister robbed the bank because he was desperate. He had made some disastrous business decisions and decided that there was only one way out."

This made me feel bad. I realized that Mr. Hollister, may his soul rest in peace, was an amateur. When it came to desperation moves there were a thousand bad ways out. The job of the truly professional desperate individual is to pick the best bad way out.

I let Ottman talk.

"He said that right after he left the bank he started to panic. He saw your cab parked in the lot, so instead of getting into his own car, which was parked in a lot next door, he decided to let the cabbie—you—become his getaway driver. He wanted to leave the scene as quickly as possible. But his panic got worse. He hadn't been in the cab one minute before he decided to back out of the whole plan. In desperation he removed the money from the briefcase and shoved it down behind the seat. He was afraid that if he was caught they would find the money in his possession, so he wanted to be carrying an empty briefcase.

"He said that after he got out of the cab, he walked into the parking lot. But his panic overtook him and he started running. He was sixty-four years old. His heart gave out."

I sat and listened to this narrative without asking the questions that kept popping up, and without making comments that would have been so gauche that faux pas didn't even begin to cover them. I wondered why French words captured stupidity so much better than English words.

So they had known about the hidden money all along. By "all along" I mean "long enough to have come around asking me pointed questions after my taxicab mysteriously burned up." With my luck, the U.S. probably had an extradition treaty with the South Pacific.

Detective Ottman slowly rose from his chair and placed a hand on my shoulder. "You did the right thing bringing that money to us, Murph. You're a good man."

I had to stop myself from calling him a liar to his face.

He took a deep breath and let it out with a sigh. "But I'm afraid I have some bad news, Murph. My partner and I had another reason for coming over here today. I'll give it to you straight. Mrs. Jacobs intends to press charges against you for assault. She's also going to sue the Rocky Mountain Taxicab Company."

I nodded. This wasn't news to me. Logic was my co-pilot—which was ironic because logic is the basis of all mathematics, my bete noir. Why am I so lousy at making change for customers and so good at predicting disaster? It defies logic.

"Her word against mine," I said.

"I'm afraid so, Murph."

"Is she still in the cardiac unit at the hospital?"

"That's right."

"Did you come here this afternoon to take me to jail?"

"No, Murph," Ottman said. "There haven't been any charges filed. Mrs. Hollister's lawyer is waiting until the medical report is in."

Quigg spoke to me. "Have you given any thought to getting yourself a lawyer?"

"No."

That's all I said. I didn't elaborate. I didn't tell him that there was no use wasting my money on a lawyer. I would go the court-appointed route and waste the taxpayer's money. I was used to doing this. I did it for two years during the army, and seven years during college, although the GI Bill only covered four year's worth of college, but somehow I managed to stretch it out to seven in total defiance of logic. I graduated from college when I was twenty-nine. I bummed around for two years before I finally started cab driving. I'm not sure if earning twenty thousand dollars a year at Dyna-Plex qualifies as "bumming"—but again, I'm not that hot with numbers.

"We're going to have to ask you to come down to headquarters and give us a statement about your discovery of the stolen money," Ottman said.

"Okay," I said. "But can you give me a few minutes? I need to talk to Mr. Hogan."

"We'll be right outside," Ottman said.

After they left, I looked at Hogan.

"That's that, isn't it," I said. It wasn't a question. It was "closure."

Hogan nodded. "I've had to keep the top brass abreast of the situation, Murph. I talked to them this afternoon before I gave you the el-two. Detectives Ottman and Quigg showed up after I told the dispatcher to call you in. I thought their visit had to do only with Mrs. Jacobs, but they told me Mr. Hollister had died." He paused a moment, then said, "It looks like you won't be driving for us anymore, Murph."

I nodded.

"I fought for you, Murph."

"I know. But it's her word against mine, and she's in the hospital."

He nodded.

"I didn't threaten her with violence," I said.

"I know."

"I did threaten to call the police, but I've done that with other fares."

"You were within your rights," he said. "It's too bad you didn't follow through with it. Pennies are not legal tender."

"Yeah. But I would never call the police on an old lady. Doing things that aren't in me is where I draw the line." I didn't mention that doing things that aren't in me takes too much effort.

"I'll need your key and trip-sheet," Hogan said.

"I know."

I handed them over. At least I didn't have to hand them over to Rollo. I stood up and turned to leave. Then I turned back and reached out and shook hands with Hogan. Mister Hogan—the best supervisor I ever had. Unlike so many foremen, bosses, and supervisors whom I had worked under during my youth, he wasn't the kind of overseer who hounded the people in his charge. In a way, Mr. Hogan was a role model for me. He always did his very best to avoid everybody he could at all times. It would be impossible to discount the influence he had over me during my career as a cab driver, and as a human being. I wanted to tell him this, but it would have contravened the very lesson he had taught me about canning small talk. Nevertheless I tried to communicate this truth to him through body language. I gave him a firm handshake and let go. It was the first time we had touched in fourteen years. The other time was the day I met him. He had a rather limpid handshake, but that was in keeping with his reticence.

I turned and walked out the door and made my way slowly down the stairwell. As I passed through the on-call room I didn't look toward the cage. I felt that my refusal to turn my head in that direction would speak volumes, i.e., "Victory—thy name is Rollo."

When I got outside, Ottman and Quigg were waiting for me. A black-and-white was parked next to 123. An unmarked unit was parked next to that. Ottman and Quigg were talking to two men, maybe detectives, but I didn't ask. One of them was taking pictures of the backseat with a large camera.

Ottman and Quigg drove me down to DPD. They escorted me to the room where I had written my first witness statement. Again, they gave me enough extra paper to hang myself. But I made it short. I decided to eschew Faulkner and embrace Hemingway. I had never been a fan of minimalism in literature, but on that day I pulled out all the stops and became a regular Raymond Carver. I didn't use the extra paper. I put it all down on the official form. The itch to fill up the last inch of blank space with more words came over me, but I fought it. It's hard to break old habits, but not that hard. I've been avoiding blank pages ever since my brother gave me the RamBlaster 4000.

A black-and-white chauffeured me back to the motor where I'd left my Chevy. I didn't recognize the cop. It had been a long time since my Chevy had been hot-wired. A whole new generation of young cops were coming along who had never knocked on my door at odd hours of the day or night to tell me that my portable dump had been found within a mile of my building.

Suddenly I felt old.

CHAPTER 22

As I drove out of the RMTC parking lot I passed a cab coming in off the day shift. A newbie was driving. I recognized him. He had driven his first shift two weeks earlier. An old pro named Jacobson had won twenty dollars in the "newbie" pool, but I'd rather not go into that.

As we passed each other, I took a good look at the kid.

Kid.

He looked thirty. But I thought to myself, "Fourteen years from now he'll be the same age I am now." Which was true in terms of experience if not age. It didn't matter whether you were thirty-five or sixty-five—if you had driven a taxi as long as I had, you were a member of my generation. We spoke the same lingo, made up the same colorful songs, and dreamed the same big dream. It didn't matter whether or not a cab driver aspired to score off writing novels someday. The true big dream of all asphalt warriors is to stop driving. You know you've conquered Everest when you can afford to park your hack for the last time.

But I never dreamed that the top of Everest would be so cold and lonely. I never dreamed that I would walk away from Rocky Cab in disgrace. Disgrace is for amateurs. But who was I to claim to be anything else? Looking back over the previous three days, I realized that disgrace was the only logical outcome. And to think that it all started by hitting the snooze button.

If I hadn't hit the snooze button, I wouldn't have shown up late for work on Monday. If I hadn't shown up late, I never would have gotten stuck in a long line at 7-11. Never would have picked up a pedestrian who gave me a twenty for a three-dollar ride. Never would have been in a position to pick up the penny lady, or the kid going to his reunion, or the Dagwell lady, or the Hobbits, never would have pulled a boneheaded blunder worthy of a tenderfoot by jumping the Chambers bell, a call so far away, so off the charts, so monumentally unrealistic that it was laughable—and thus never would have found myself standing in front an armed and desperate man at the Glendale Bank & Trust.

And that was just Monday.

How about Tuesday?

If I hadn't hit the snooze button I never would have found myself in front of the penny lady's front door at seven-thirty in the morning, never would have threatened to call the police on a woman who was probably living on a fixed income and had concocted a scheme to avoid paying cab fares that was so brilliant it was worthy of me. I couldn't begin to tell you some of the crap I've pulled in my life. My two years in the army alone would fill the *Encyclopedia of Goldbricking*.

And now it had caught up with me at last. But the funny thing was, even though I knew "it" had been pursuing me all my life, I had never really known what "it" was. But on the day that I found myself driving home from Rocky Cab for the last time ever I realized exactly what "it" was: justice.

I deserved a nickel in the slammer.

That's what I told myself as I guided my heap along the mean streets of Denver toward The Hill. I deserved two of those years for the lie of omission that I had committed in front of Ottman and Quigg that afternoon. "You're a good man, Murph."

It put me off my feed.

And then there were all the "bad" thoughts I had reveled in concerning Mrs. Jacobs, who was lying in a ward at DGH with tubes and wires attached to her feeble frame. And how about all the "bad" thoughts I would have invented for Mr. Hollister if he hadn't died? Oh yeah. I wasn't kidding myself. I had the senior citizens of Denver in my rifle sights that week. One down and one to go. And for all I knew, Mrs. Jacobs was already dead.

I deserved a seat on Ol' Sparky.

I headed for a Burger King where I intended to pick up dinner. I didn't feel like cooking for myself that night. That was how I normally rewarded myself if I did something unexpectedly right. I celebrated by going commercial, with a side order of fries. I once tried to boil frozen French-fries in a saucepan at home, but let's move on.

I had all but pulled into the burger joint drive-up lane when I changed my mind. My feed had not come back, and I never could abide eating cold commercial hamburgers, which was what I would have ended up with if I had bought some and taken them home and not eaten them right away. And cold French fries were beyond the pale. So I bypassed the drive-up lane and headed home. No. If my feed ever came back, I was going to force myself to take the Daniel Boone route: If you want to eat, then you're going to have to catch it, kill it, and cook it yourself, pilgrim.

I had pretty much finished berating myself by the time I pulled into the parking lot behind my crow's nest. I guided my Chevy into the choice V-spot, then shut off the engine. I sat in the silence of The Hill thinking about the thing I had been avoiding thinking about ever since I had heard Detective Ottman say, "Mr. Hollister confessed that he had stuffed the money down behind the backseat of the taxi that he had ridden in on the day he robbed the Glendale Bank & Trust."

If I had gone through with my plan of figuring out a way to steal the one-hundred thousand dollars, there was no question that I would already be in jail. But did that scare me? Not as much as the fact that I had seriously considered trying to pull it off. I had examined it from every angle, and the plan had seemed flawless. All it would have taken would be the death of Mr. Hollister. And after I learned that he had died, it was as if Fate had taken me by the hand and shown me the way to Tahiti.

That's what really scared me.

There was somebody inside of me that I had never met before: Me.

That was the only name I had for it. As good a name as any, and better than most.

I reached up and took hold of the rear-view mirror and turned it so I could see my eyes.

I stared at those eyes.

I stared long and hard.

I stared until I fully understood that if it hadn't been for sheer luck I would be staring at iron bars.

But I wasn't.

I was sitting in my Chevy on The Hill, having what I could only describe as a very bad epiphany.

Except, had it been sheer luck? I tried to mentally trace the timeline of my movements back to the moment when I had found the money in my taxi. I had been parked in this very spot. I had taken the money upstairs, then fiddled around for God only knew how long, pretending I was going to call the police, and had finally slipped into a surreal, dreamlike state where I had extrapolated upon a means by which I could flee the country a wealthy man. And then ... and then ...

And then what happened?

Then I remembered.

The telephone rang.

The ringing had snapped me out of it.

I had been saved by a goddamn telephone!

I climbed out of my car and locked the doors, even though locked doors meant nothing to car thieves. I guess I locked it to keep out the good people. I climbed the fire escape to my crow's nest, went inside, set my briefcase on the kitchen table, and walked into the living room. I looked at my answering machine. No messages. The auto-answer was off. I pressed the button turning it back on. I waited.

Nothing happened.

I was sort of hoping the telephone would immediately ring. That's what it normally did when I didn't want it to. If it rang though, I was going to do something I could not remember doing in a long time. I was going to pick up the receiver before the answering machine kicked in. I was going to listen to the sales spiel of the telemarketer. The odds of it being a telemarketer were well above 90 percent. The odds of it being a friend were zero. Of course odds have nothing to do with reality, which is why so many people go home sad from the dog track.

But if it had been a telemarketer on the other end of the line I was going to ask whether he had called earlier, and if it turned out that he was the capitalist who had snapped me out of my crime spree, I would thank him for saving me from going to Cañon City for a minimum of five years with time off for behavior so good that the screws would wonder if I actually was innocent. I have a theory that jailhouse guards do not spend a lot of time wondering that about prisoners.

Having disposed of the Hollister Case, I now turned my attention to the latest charges against me: the assault on Mrs. Jacobs.

Her word against mine.

The prosecution rested.

I thought about cooking a hamburger, but my feed had not come back because I had too many "important" things to think about. First of all, I had to find a job. On top of that, I was going to jail. It occurred to me that they sort of canceled each other out. But then I realized that while going to jail canceled out getting a job, getting a job did not cancel out going to jail. I wondered if there was an algebraic basis for this truth. The words, "inverse," "obverse," and "converse" came to mind, but I couldn't remember what any of them meant. For some reason they made me think of tennis shoes.

Well—I didn't have a job, I wasn't hungry, and I wasn't in jail, so there was only one thing to do: collapse onto my mattress. No use worrying about tomorrow. The happiest people I know live unexamined lives.

That night I dreamed I was walking through a mall that resembled the Cherry Creek Shopping Center. I was trying to find a store, but I couldn't remember what store, or what I wanted to buy. When I woke up, I couldn't help but marvel at what a mediocre subconscious I have. I looked at the alarm clock. It was a few minutes after four a.m. I had slept for ten hours. I was bothered by the fact that I had not slept fitfully. Given the rigidly defined parameters of my immediate future, an objective observer might have concluded that I was out of touch with reality. But mostly I was hungry. That's the stomach for you—the phoniest organ in the human body. It runs away when things are going badly, but it always returns when it wants something.

I almost threw the covers off my bed, but managed to stop myself in time. I didn't want to knock over my lamp and blow a fuse in the building and go downstairs and wake the manager to tell him that everybody's digital alarm clocks weren't going to buzz on time.

I got as dressed as I ever do, then went into the kitchen and opened the refrigerator and looked at my food. I don't want to describe the contents of my refrigerator. You heard me right: plurals. I did have more than one content on the shelves, even though I was a bachelor. Two of them were eggs. I decided to boil them in a pan of water, and then walk down the block and pick up a copy of the *Denver Post*.

It was that time again, a time known to all bachelors of all ages, but mostly young bachelors. It was time to look at the want-ads and see if there was anything listed that I might possibly be able to do to get money. Of course I rarely found jobs in the want-ads, but reading the ads was like priming the pump. The next step would be to go down to the state employment agency, which was as close as you could get to reality without actually being there. I had never gotten a job through any state employment agency, and that included Pennsylvania, although I had heard rumors. The real way you got jobs was through your friends. Unfortunately I didn't have any friends. It depressed me to know that if I was going to find a job, I would have to tap into my vast network of enemies. They loved to see me work.

I put the eggs in the pan to boil, then I stepped outside and went down the fire escape and walked through the pre-dawn darkness to the corner and bought a newspaper. I'll admit it. If there was any way I could have stolen a newspaper I would have done it. I admitted it to myself as I stood there jiggling the door open and closed before inserting a quarter. Face it. Any man who would go to unusual lengths to plan the heist of one-hundred thousand dollars would have no qualms about stealing a newspaper. I was the living embodiment of pure evil and I knew it.

I walked back to my crow's nest thinking about the fact that if it wasn't so cold in the Arctic I wouldn't mind living in a place that was dark half the year. During the bright summer months I could move down to the Antarctic. I wondered who the genius was who named the Antarctic.

When I got back upstairs, my eggs were boiling. I set my morning paper on the table, then pulled a dish out of the cupboard and crushed some saltines onto the plate. I cracked open the soft-boiled eggs and poured them onto the saltines. I grabbed a soda from the fridge and sat down at the table. Bachelor breakfast. Married women don't know what they're missing.

I scooped up a spoonful of egg-on-cracker and shoveled it into my mouth, then I looked at the front page of the *Post*.

And started choking.

CHAPTER 23

"Cab Driver Questioned In Assault."

I took a quick swallow of soda and washed down the crackers, then I held the *Post* closer and began reading an article at the bottom right-hand corner.

"Rocky Mountain Taxicab driver Brendan Murphy is currently under investigation for the assault of a seventy-one-year-old widow, Mrs. Emma Jacobs, who claims he threatened her life after she attempted to pay a cab fare with pennies. The woman is currently being treated at the DGH cardiac unit after suffering a heart attack following the assault."

I read the story twice, especially the part that said "following the assault."

I assumed that this was what people meant by being tried and convicted by the news media. I felt like getting angry, however it just didn't seem worth the effort. At least newspapers didn't have the authority to sentence people to jail. That was up to the readers. This made me think of writing a novel about a country where people were tried and convicted by journalists. "Write what you know about," they say.

But this didn't seem worth the effort either. It made me feel bad because my brother Gavin must have spent a fortune on the RamBlaster 4000 and I wasn't using it to write novels. I had fooled around with the word processor long enough to understand that there had never been a machine devised that made it so hard to avoid writing. All my excuses were gone. No carbon papers to wrestle with, and no bottles of Wite-Out to cover up those typos. I've always wondered if Mike Nesmith's mother took a financial hit after the word processor was invented.

But the best part about the computer was not having to retype manuscripts. It took me forever to type a second draft of a novel back when I was using my Smith Corona portable typewriter. By "forever" I mean "six months." But now I could make changes and print out a whole book in one weekend, if I ever got around to writing a book. I wondered if the paper industry took a hit after the invention of the computer. Surely novelists were using less paper than before, although they probably were using more electricity. In theory it all evened out, since according to the conspiracy theorists at Rocky Cab, all the business enterprises in the entire world are owned by one big secret organization—which means that ruling the world is like driving a taxi: you never win, and you never lose.

Well, those days were gone. It was time to look for a new job, although I just needed something to tide me over until I went to jail. I could have said to hell with it and stayed unemployed until my trial came up, but I didn't want the screws in the big house to think I was a loafer. From what little I knew about the penal system, it wasn't like the army. It's true that getting arrested had surface similarities to getting drafted, especially if you were innocent. But unlike sergeants, you couldn't put anything over on the screws. They were hip to the cons. Most of my sergeants weren't even hip to Pat Boone much less Janis.

The journey through the want-ads ultimately put me into the proper frame of mind, so I decided to drive down to the state employment agency and see what they had to offer a forty-five-year-old man who possessed no marketable skills—in other words, an English major.

By then it was six o'clock in the morning. It was unusual to be awake at this hour on a Thursday. My biological clock was so finely tuned that I always woke up at six-thirty on Monday, Wednesday, and Friday. Whereas I woke up at ten a.m. on Tuesday, Thursday, Saturday, and Sunday. It had taken fourteen years of fine-tuning my brain to get it to understand that it didn't have to think on Monday, Wednesday, and Friday. But those days were over.

Cab driving was the only job I ever had that allowed me to pick and choose the days I would work. It was similar to college where I was allowed to pick and choose the days I would attend classes, which ironically were also M-W-F. I took Tuesdays and Thursdays off in college, unless there was a required class that I absolutely could not get out of. But even then I usually managed to find a class that didn't begin until one in the afternoon. It could be a real struggle. I always thought of registration day as Hell Week.

Due to the fact that the state employment agency wouldn't open up until I was mentally ready to look for work, I turned on the TV without any hope that I would find an episode of *Gilligan's Island.* There had been a period in my life when six o'clock in the morning was a bleak time to look for TV shows. But thanks to the technological godsend of the co-axial cable, six o'clock in the morning was like any other time of day. It was almost as if cable television had brought Time itself to a halt, forcing everything to happen all at once. Science fiction was being overtaken by reality, although I doubted that sci-fi would ever actually be bypassed, because just when the bright boys with their Ph.D.s from M.I.T. produced everything conceived originally by speculative fiction writers, some trekkie with a Smith Corona would think up one more teensy little scientific concept that would send the academics dashing back to their slide-rulers in a fit of pique. Take Teflon for instance. And Tang. Just two examples of the superiority of novelists over NASA.

But I had never found a *Gilligan's* at this hour of the day. It made me wonder what was wrong with the minds of cable executives. Lotta money being lost there, as far as I was concerned, although I didn't actually know how programming *Gilligan's Island* at this hour would increase their profits—but it was the principle of the thing. In the best of all possible worlds, Mary Ann would be accessible to cable subscribers throughout the world 24/7. I thought about writing an angry letter.

Instead, I surfed for an hour, and only came up for air when I started colliding with commercials on the broadcast stations, which are like reefs in the cable sea. It was seven a.m.

True, it was Thursday, but I still felt as if I should be at work, checking 123 for dents and dings, and staying away from the radiator cap. I ought to have made a personal vow a long time ago to never again as long as I lived pop a hood, but sometimes you can't avoid pretending to check the engine, especially when a cab breaks down with fares in the backseat. A couple minutes of leaning meaninglessly under the hood eats up some of the waiting time for the tow truck.

And then, at seven fifteen, the phone rang.

I was almost enraged. The idea that anybody would phone me at this ungodly hour made me grit my teeth, but then I realized that people called my answering machine at this hour with regularity, and it never mattered because I was either at work or asleep. But things were different now. I grabbed the phone off the hook because I wanted to thank the telemarketer who had snapped me out of my reverie on Wednesday. Any proxy would do. It's the thought that counts as the Hallmark people have made more than adequately clear.

"Hello?" I said.

There was a moment of silence at the other end of the line.

"Murph?" a voice said.

My shoulders drooped. I was instantly filled with regret. Strangers I can handle, but people who know my name—

Jaysus.

"Yes?" I said.

"Is this Brendan Murphy?"

"Yes?"

"What are you doing answering your telephone?"

My entire universe drooped. This was why I never answered my telephone.

"It rang," I said. As good an answer as any, and better than most.

"This is Hogan. I'm sorry if I woke you up."

"Oh … no problem, Mr. Hogan," I lied indirectly. I wanted to keep my options open.

"Listen, Murph, you have to get down to the motor right away."

"I do?"

"Yes."

"But I don't work for Rocky anymore."

"Listen, Murph, this is very important. You know that I would never call you at home if I could avoid it."

"I know. Does it have anything to do with the police?"

"Yes."

"Okay. But … in that case why haven't the police called me?"

"I can't explain it over the phone, Murph. You have to come here in person."

"Okay. Give me twenty minutes."

We rang off.

Right then and there I made a personal vow that if I was ever locked inside a safe at the bottom of the Marianas Trench I would have an answering machine.

I started to gather up my cab accoutrement, then I realized that I was a victim of habit. I realized it when I reached for my copy of *Lolita.* I didn't need any starting cash. If I was lucky, Hogan was luring me down to Rocky so the police could toss a net and haul me off with a minimum of fuss.

I left my starting cash in *Lolita,* left my Rocky cap and jacket in the closet, and left my briefcase on the table. I closed up my crow's nest and walked down the fire escape, glancing around the neighborhood for cops. After all, if I was going to trap me out in the open, I would make a fake call from Hogan, then dry-gulch me as soon as I came out the door.

I made it to my Chevy with a minimum of difficulty, got in, and started the engine, thinking how ironic it would be if my car had been stolen overnight. Very convenient, eh? It might have looked to the police as if I "knew" something was up. I rarely get the chance to look as if I know anything.

As I drove to Rocky I wondered if they had found something else under the backseat of 123, like a corpse.

The viaducts came into view. I never thought I would see them again—not counting normal driving in this part of town. I started to feel funny as I approached Rocky Cab. You would understand how I felt if you had spent fourteen years doing nothing on three out of every four Thursdays. As I say, my brain is finely tuned, is as sensitive to the subtle changes in my personal atmosphere as a barometer is attuned to the subtle changes of whatever the hell affects it. Air pressure, I guess. I wonder what Torricelli did for a living when he wasn't inventing stuff for sea captains.

I turned left onto the street that led to the parking lot, and that's when things started to get real strange. There were cabs lining both sides of the road, and not just Rocky Cabs but Yellow Cabs and Metro Cabs and Checkers and a couple other representatives from companies that have since gone belly-up so there's no reason to name names. With all the different colors and body markings, it looked like the cabstand at DIA.

I slowed to a crawl, wondering if by some chance a group of cabbies from one of the companies had at last realized a career-long dream and had convinced every taxi driver in Denver to go on strike for higher meter rates and lower lease payments. If so, I was ready to keep driving until I hit Wichita.

But I turned into the lot. Hogan had given me an artificial L-2, and

I was going to see it through to the bitter end. I didn't have much hope of finding a parking space. It looked like every driver who worked for Rocky was present. But then I saw Big Al standing near the door to the on-call room. He gave me the high sign and pointed to an empty space near the door. I gave him a thumbs-up and drove toward it, but then I hit the brakes.

Wait a minute.

The odds of finding an empty space in a situation like this were three hundred to one, whereas the odds of Big Al directing me to that space were the same as winning the lottery—one in five trillion. Somebody was up to something, and for the first time in my memory it wasn't me.

When he saw me hit the brakes, Big Al shook his head with what an objective observer might interpret as disgust, but which I interpreted as understanding. He marched across the lot and came up to my window.

"Can the paranoia, Tenderfoot," he said. "Just pull into the space that I saved for you without any thought of personal gain on my part."

That was good enough for me. When it came to self-aggrandizement, Big Al didn't fool around.

I pulled into the parking space and shut off the engine. By that time Hogan had come out the door. He was holding a newspaper in one hand. He walked toward me.

I climbed out ready to face the music. By "ready" I mean "resigned." I'm never ready for anything.

Then I noticed something truly weird. A group of cabbies, one from each different company, fell in behind Hogan as he approached. I hadn't seen a show of unity like this since *The Ox-Bow Incident*.

"Thanks for coming in, Murph," Hogan said. Then he reached out and shook my hand. I couldn't believe it. We had touched three times in fourteen years.

"Murph, everybody here has read the story about you in the newspaper. Big Al brought me a copy of the paper this morning. In fact, it was

Big Al who called all these drivers together. They asked me to call you and request that you come down here today."

"Why?" I said.

"Because they didn't want to go to your apartment."

"I understand," I said.

He pointed at Big Al. "Maybe you'd like to do the talking."

"'Like' isn't the word," Big Al said, but he stepped forward anyway. He took the newspaper from Hogan and held it up so I could see my story. He slapped it with the backs of his fingertips.

"Well Tenderfoot, I might have known you would be the man to expose the dirty little secret of every cab driver in Denver," he said without preamble. "Every driver present today has been defrauded by this woman at some time in the past. During whispered conversations she is referred to as 'The Penny Lady.' But nobody has ever had the guts to step forward and admit publicly that he had been taken to the cleaners by this … this … well, let's just say 'grandmotherly female.' It was too humiliating. It was something you just didn't talk about. Not even me … and you know me. I've spent the past fourteen years mocking your ineptitude and your stunning lack of personal growth."

I nodded. What could I say?

"But thanks to you, greenhorn, the secret is out. We no longer have to bear our burden of shame. Not one man here believes that you threatened this woman with physical violence. During the past fourteen years most of us have watched you scramble hopelessly to make an honest buck, because that's the only buck you'll ever make. You don't have a dishonest bone in your body, Murph, and you would never harm a living creature. To put it bluntly—you're all talk."

I hung my head with humility. These guys had me pegged.

"That's why I put out the word this morning. After I saw this story I told every man-jack in the Denver cab fleet that the time had come to take a stand and bring this … this … well … this grandmotherly female to her knees and make her grovel for mercy. Right now we're going to form a parade of taxis and drive to DGH where she is no doubt pretending to be suffering from a heart attack in order to gain sympathy from the general public and strengthen her lawyer's bogus case against you."

He stopped.

He had said all he had to say.

A silence fell over the dirt lot.

I looked at Big Al, looked at the Hogan, looked at the cabbies from all the different companies who were gathered around in a circle so large that it was more like a scene from *Hang 'Em High*.

"I don't know what to say," I said, getting choked up. "I thought none of you guys liked me. Especially you Yellow drivers who bet on me that time I went to LA."

There were a few discreet coughs and a shuffling of feet, then Big Al spoke up. "It's the principle of the thing, Murph. That's what you need to keep at the forefront of your mind. The odds of anybody here ever liking you dwindle in comparison to the broader concept of justice served."

I was relieved when he said that. For one moment I feared I was going to be burdened with hundreds of new friends.

I raised my chin and looked at the drivers and said, "Thank you." Raymond Carver couldn't have said it shorter.

But then I realized I actually could have said it shorter by saying, "Thanks." Damn. I would have said that if I had thought of it in time, but my mouth had spoken before my brain had performed any copy-editing. Well, there was no revising in the real world, but nevertheless I would have just said "Thanks" if I could have done it over again, which I couldn't, but wished I could have, darn it anyway.

I felt a psychological tic coming on.

CHAPTER 24

Does this story have a happy ending? That depends on your definition of "story." Maybe the reason I'm an unpublished novelist is that I have a hard time keeping my stories straight—as good an excuse as any, and about the same as most. I would like to blame it on the fact that I own a computer, but I think I've already made mincemeat out of that excuse. My only hope is to shoot down all of my excuses, which will leave me with no alternative except to sit down in front of my RamBlaster, but let's move on.

I don't know how many cabs took part in the parade of taxis that made its way to downtown Denver. My guess would be seventy, about the same number of cabs that sit idle at DIA on any given day. Big Al led the parade in his vintage cab, #61. This annoyed me because I felt I ought to have been the one to lead the parade. But I guess his insatiable ego made him think he was more important than me. That'll be the day.

By the time we passed the Capitol building, half of the DPD black-and-white units were escorting us with their red lights flashing. It made me feel cool until they blocked us off at 11th Avenue and pulled out tear-gas guns. I don't suppose it is necessary for me to explain to you my misinterpretation of the facts.

It was at this point that Big Al graciously stepped aside to let me take charge of the explanations. By the time I got finished name-dropping Ottman and Quigg and Duncan and Argyle, the other cab drivers had fled the scene.

To my knowledge no cabbies were apprehended for anything, but the event did garner a thirty-second report on a local TV channel that evening. Denver has somewhat of a reputation as a "slow-news" town.

To his credit, Big Al did accompany me the rest of the way to DGH in order to confront the lawyer representing Mrs. Jacobs, and to pick up a fare at the outpatient clinic. He had jumped the bell on the way to the hospital, the bastard.

Two hours after the parade of taxis was stopped by the police, the accusations against me were withdrawn by Mrs. Jacobs' lawyer. I assume he consulted her, but from what I know about lawyers I shouldn't speculate on the motives of people who share in the profits of litigation. And anyway, I prefer to focus on the human side of things. From what I know about lawyers, that shouldn't take long.

What a week. When I wasn't staring at the portrait of Dorian Gray in my bathroom mirror, I nearly bit my tongue in half trying to keep from calling people liars to their faces. After Big Al told me I didn't have a dishonest bone in my body, I realized I had been giving him too much credit all these years. Apparently he couldn't read me like an X-ray after all. He was good with body language, probably better than me, and in all humility I have to say that's a fairly remarkable achievement. But still, I had lived most of my adult life with the belief that everybody could see right through me. Also my teenage years, as well as my childhood years. Authority figures had something to do with this. Also my vivid imagination. Case in point: a bathroom mirror with a towel draped over it, but I don't want to talk about that.

Ever since the day Mrs. Jacobs was brought to her knees and forced to admit that I had never threatened her with physical violence, I've been doing a lot of thinking. I've been thinking about all the things I think about when I have epiphanies, whether in my taxi, in front of my TV, or in a bathtub, usually mine. My bathtub ranks numero uno in the epiphany department. Maybe it's because I'm almost always naked when I take a bath and feel completely exposed. I know I shouldn't think about old ladies when I'm naked, but when I've got a washcloth draped over my eyes and I'm humming "… singing in the rain …" my mind sort of drifts in random directions. Thus, the cognizant part of me that perceives thoughts is able browse around like I'm channel-surfing an organic coaxial-cable.

Question: What is the largest organ of the human body?

Answer: The skin.

I heard that on *Hollywood Squares.*

That's the kind of thought I have when I'm meditating in the bathtub. It's similar to the kinds of thoughts I have all the time. This leads me to believe that I've always lived in a state of cosmic consciousness, minus the wisdom. But maybe the lack of wisdom explains why I don't grasp a lot of things. Back in high school I never paid attention to the teacher during algebra class. I never paid attention to any teachers. I spent most of my time paying attention to normal things. At least I thought they were normal. Little did I realize that watching five hundred organic channels during every waking moment was not normal. I'm using the word "normal" in reference to the entire human race. Almost nobody else daydreams eighteen out of twenty-four hours a day. In my case it would be twelve out of twelve, but for the sake of argument I'll pretend to be normal.

As I soaked in my bathtub on Thursday evening I started thinking about Mrs. Jacobs, and how awful it would be to spend your life trying to cut corners on a fixed income by defrauding cabbies and everybody else capable of being fooled. I thought of the guts it would take to do such a thing. The only other woman I knew with guts like that was my Maw. She didn't even fear nuns. So I guess I take after me ol' Dad in that respect. He matriculated in the St. Louis parochial school system, reputed to be the most rugged educational program in the country—including Baltimore, where the Catechism comes from. Even Protestant kids are intimidated by "Big Lou."

But me ol' mither never relied on a bucketful of pennies to "supplement" her household income. The lowest she ever sank, as far as I know, was stealing fifty dollars from me after I pulled a Santa gig last Christmas. It's a long story, but given the fact that she had waited on me hand-and-foot for more than twenty years, I had decided to let that slide. It's true that she charged me for meals after I got a paper route, and kept a running tab until I left home, but that was just business and not personal. She made me an offer I couldn't refuse: free room and TV as long as the GI Bill kept rolling in. I was a fool to have left home before I graduated from WSU. I was a fool to have left WSU itself. I was a fool to have told Mary Margaret Flaherty I wanted to be a novelist. I should have told her I wanted to be a railroad brakeman. Wichita girls are easy—to get past third base all you have to do is tell them the only thing you want out of life is to trudge to work every day with a lunch bucket—the coach will wave you home with a resounding "Slide! Slide!"

Well … that was water under the bridge.

But I couldn't stop thinking about Mrs. Jacobs. Sure, she had defrauded me and every other cab driver in Denver to the tune of thousands of dollars over the years, and sure, she had faked a heart attack in order to swindle a fortune out of Rocky Cab, but how did that make her any different from me?

This was what I thought about as I reclined in my bathtub that evening, watching random cable shows but always hitting the "last" button on the remote and coming back to the show I called "The Penny Lady" starring Mrs. Jacobs. I once read a letter to the editor from a woman demanding to know when Channel 2 was going to start showing repeats of *Hazel.* I don't know why I bring that up.

But the thought of Mrs. Jacobs puttering around that old Denver house not three miles from where I lived made me think of all the old people in America whose lives were fenced-in by fixed incomes. It made me think of all the people in America whose lives were lived devoid of hope. But it also made me think of all the people in America whose lives were blessed with a hope that they never tapped into because they spent half their time lying in bathtubs feeling sorry for themselves instead of sitting in front of their word processors banging out novels. It made me think of how utterly worthless I was, and how wrong everybody had been about me.

Every nice thing that every cop and cabbie had said about me during the past week had been grounded in appalling misconceptions. They were judging me based on my actions because they couldn't see inside me, couldn't read me like an X-ray, couldn't witness first-hand the living embodiment of pure evil that roamed the mean streets of Denver. But that was probably a good thing.

Maybe actions are the only things that really count in this world.

This was what I thought about as I hummed the best of Gene Kelly.

Maybe it didn't matter that I was the living embodiment of pure evil, as long as I was polite to old people and paid my rent on time, two things that I always did. Maybe I took my brain too seriously. Maybe I should stop thinking so much and sit down in front of my RamBlaster and move my fingers more than my mouth. I had written an awful lot of novels with my mouth, especially down at Sweeney's. Maybe the time had come to stop feeling sorry for myself.

I didn't hold out much hope.

The last time I tried to reform myself, I gave two-hundred and fifty dollars to a jock in Danskins and visited the gym twice before giving up. Was it the sore muscles that had sent me tumbling into the bottomless pit of despair? No. It was instant gratification—or the lack of it. After two sessions with the barbells I expected to look like Sandow. He was the world's first famous bodybuilder. He was a featured attraction in Ziegfeld's Follies during the 1890s. I know this because he was portrayed in *The Great Ziegfeld* (1936) starring William Powell and Myrna Loy. What a couple. When they weren't wowing audiences on the *Great White Way,* they were solving crimes on the mean streets of San Francisco. When did they ever find time to mix martinis?

After I had gotten home on Thursday afternoon, Hogan called to tell me everything was copacetic with the top brass and I could come back to work. That's what started me thinking. That's what sent me to the bathtub. I wasn't sure I wanted to go back to work.

But I did return to work on Friday morning. This is one of the drawbacks of thinking: it causes you to assess things. I had no job, and I had earned no money that week. In theory I can pick up one hundred and fifty dollars in profit if I work hard on any given Friday, and that isn't an exaggeration. Big All does it in preparation for going to Vegas to "clear out the cobwebs." All it takes is hard work.

I've pretty much listed the drawback to hard work, but I don't think I've ever really elaborated on the benefits. You heard me right: plurals. But maybe that's because there is no plurals. You heard me right: is. The only benefit to hard work is money. If you know of another one, keep it to yourself. I've got more motivation than I can handle.

When I walked into the on-call room on Friday, nobody paid any attention to me. I liked that. Rollo was sitting in the cage, an eclair drying on a saucer at his elbow. He was too busy handing out keys and trip-sheets to give me more than a cursory glare.

I took my key and trip-sheet and walked out to the parking lot where Rocky Mountain Taxicab #123 was waiting for me. The backseat was in place. The garage mechanics must have done it. I don't know about you, but I have never been able to lock a backseat into place by myself. It's like fiddling with a stuck drawer.

I didn't have to check the body for dents and dings because I had been the last person to use it. I stayed away from the radiator cap, got behind the wheel, signed on, and drove out of there.

I got gassed and snacked at 7-11, then drove straight to the Brown Palace where I parked fourth in line at the cabstand. I set up shop, opened my paperback, and commenced to getting things back to normal. I had no intention of working hard. I intended to earn my daily fifty and go home. I intended to put the past behind me, which wasn't hard because that's where it is anyway. An hour later a businessman climbed into the backseat and said, "DIA." When we got there he gave me sixty bucks and told me to keep it. I had been on duty for an hour-and-a-half, and I had earned almost half my daily take.

This is the kind of score that motivates cabbies to work hard. Pretty soon you start thinking that if you could earn sixty dollars every hour-and-a-half you would make a lot of money. How much money I don't know because I'm not good at math, which has proven irrelevant in my life.

After I dropped him off I drove down to the DIA cabstand and looked at the seventy or so taxis waiting in line for one of their two potential trips out of DIA. If any of them were able to get more than two trips, they knew more than I did. But three trips might be the big dream of cabbies that don't write novels. I don't see much difference between sitting in a taxi at DIA or sitting in front of a word processor, although I prefer to fail big-time. I once fancied I would get a million-dollar advance for a novel—but just to inject some reality into this fantasy, I never dared to dream bigger.

I deadheaded back to Denver after that. I kept the Rocky radio off. When I got back to midtown I looked over the cabstands like a man examining suits on a dry-cleaning rack, then chose the Hilton. There were four cabs ahead of me. Plenty of time to finish my paperback and get started on a new one.

By the time I was second in line, Big Al pulled up behind me and beeped his horn. This was out of character for him. Horn beeping is the mark of a newbie. I could only conclude that it was a sarcastic beep. Big Al possesses the unique ability to turn the most innocuous gesture into a scathing denunciation. He's my hero.

I got out and walked back to RMT #61, the oldest cab in the fleet. A tip-sheet from the Mile-Hi Kennel Club lay open on the shotgun seat beside him.

"How are the dogs running?" I said.

"I can't win for losing," he replied. This was a flat-out lie. Big Al just doesn't like people to know how much he wins, especially broke people. "I wondered whether you would be working today," he said.

"Who says I'm working?"

"Touché."

"I just picked up sixty bucks on a DIA run," I bragged.

"Sweet."

We were talking cab-talk. This is what cabbies are doing when you see them flapping their jaws at a hotel stand. They're talking about their latest big score or their latest no-show, i.e., they're either bragging or complaining. It's true that some of them are discussing the secret conspiracy of a handful of ultra-rich fanatics who want to take complete control of the economic system of our planet, but it eventually drifts back to no-shows. That's because the number two rule of talking is just like the number two rule of writing: talk what you know about. The number one rule of writing is, of course: don't bore the reader. But you don't need to be a cab driver to bore a listener. I've been bored by college professors, bankers, and strippers. But then they weren't trying to make a million dollars by not boring their audience. They were just killing time. As I say, not so different from writing.

"I heard that the lawsuit was called off," Big Al said, easing into the subject that he wished to discuss. He usually cuts to the chase, but I guess things were different now that he had admitted to possessing at least one shameful secret.

"Yeah," I said, squinting in the sunlight and glancing around, checking the street for pedestrians. Two more taxis pulled into line behind Big Al.

"So tell me," he said. "Do you feel that you rightfully deserved to be let off the hook?"

"Of course not," I said. "Why do you ask?"

"Habit."

I nodded.

A man came out of the Hilton and got into the first cab in line. The other drivers started their engines in preparation for driving forward one space. The hired cab pulled away from the curb and drove down the street, leaving an empty space in front of #123.

"I guess I better pull forward," I said.

"I guess you better, Murph."

I glanced down at Big Al. Things were different now. I didn't like that.

"Who are you calling 'Murph'?" I said. "My name is 'Tenderfoot'."

Big Al smiled at me. It was a smile that spoke volumes, a smile that said, "Nothing has changed, and nothing ever will."

"Get moving, Tenderfoot," Big Al said, "before everybody starts yelling at you again."

I looked toward the entrance of the Hilton Hotel. The doorman was frowning at the unsightly empty space at the curb. I sauntered toward 123, utilizing a variety of fraudulent facial and arm movements to convince him that I was in a hurry to maintain the perfection of his area of operations.

The doorman seemed satisfied by my obsequious performance. He clasped his hands behind his back and began rocking on his heels.

I opened the driver's door to Rocky Mountain Taxicab #123. Just before I climbed in to pull forward one space, I paused and looked back at Big Al. He was already leafing through his tip-sheet.

"See you on the asphalt," I said.

"Not if I see you first," he replied.

I think he meant it.

He usually does.

The End

PICKUP AT
UNION STATION

BOOK 7 IN
THE ASPHALT WARRIOR
SERIES

COMING SOON

CHAPTER 1

I was sitting inside my taxi outside the Oxford Hotel when a call came over the radio for a pickup at Union Station. I had just dropped off a fare at the hotel, which is half a block away from the train depot. It was six-thirty Wednesday evening, it was April, and it was raining buckets. Don't ask me how the word "it" can be so all-inclusive, but it is. I guess that's the magic of language, but I didn't have time to parse the baffling splendor of the King's English because I had thirty minutes to drive my cab back to the Rocky Mountain Taxicab Company (RMTC) before my shift ended. I also had two seconds to deliberate taking the call. If I waited three seconds, another cabbie might jump the bell. The weather was so inclement that cabbies all over Denver were reaping the whirlwind. By this I mean that people were calling for taxis, so it was a seller's market and I was one of the rip-off artists on duty that night.

I caved in fast. Union Station was thirty seconds away and I have an uncontrollable craving for money. Money is like all of my uncontrollable cravings—it makes me do things I sometimes regret, although the regret usually takes place after the craving has been slaked and I'm sitting around idly thinking about nothing. Ironically I sometimes find myself regretting not having slaked a craving. If you go on dates, you probably know what I mean.

"One-twenty-three!" I said, grabbing the microphone off the dashboard.

"Union Station, party named Zelner," the dispatcher said.

"Check." I hung up the mike and made an illegal U-turn on 16th

Street. To my knowledge "illegal" is the only kind of U-turns they have in downtown Denver.

I drove across Wynkoop Street and into the driveway that fronts Union Station. Coincidentally the driveway is shaped like a U. I figured the customer for someone who had just gotten off the Zephyr coming from either Chicago or Oakland. I once rode the Zephyr to Oakland. So did Jack Kerouac but not at the same time. I pulled up at the cabstand and peered through the pouring rain toward the front door of the station, hoping the fare would be standing by the entrance waiting anxiously for his ride. Not that I like it when people are anxious, but it hurries things along.

I had my fingers crossed that the fare would ask me to take him to one of the big hotels in midtown—the Fairmont or the Hilton. I might pick up a fast five bucks and still have time to make it back to the cab company before my shift ran out. The trip would come to only two bucks or so, but people tip like madmen when it rains, especially when their taxis show up fast.

I had shown up fast. Maybe too fast. I sat staring through the wet windshield toward the front door of the terminal. The wipers were going back and forth but the rain was coming down so hard that they were virtually useless, like everything else in my life not counting TV.

I didn't see anybody.

This made me anxious. It meant I might have to get out of my cab and go into Union Station and look around for my customer. On the upside I would get to yell "Rocky Cab!" at the top of my lungs, which I have done before in the terminal. I enjoy that. My voice echoes off the high ceiling and makes me feel like a railroad conductor. I wanted to become a conductor the first time I hollered "Rocky Cab!" in the terminal but by the time I got back into my cab the ambition had faded, like most of my ambitions. If you've ever seen Grand Central Station in New York

City, Union Station is sort of like that, in the way that Denver is sort of like a city.

But I had one problem that night. If I walked into Union Station I would get wet. As I said, it was "raining buckets." Normally I don't employ clichés but I have learned over the years that people respond more readily to clichés than to James Joyce, who once took an entire page to make it clear to his readers that it was snowing all the hell over everything in Ireland. Okay Jimbo, we get the point, but where's the plot?

Aaah, don't get me started on James Joyce.

My anxiety increased. I could feel my left hand reaching for the door handle. But I kept staring at the brightly lit doorway of the terminal trying to "will" my customer to appear with a suitcase. Cab drivers do this frequently. The only thing besides the rain that stopped me from getting out and rushing toward the terminal was the fact that I had gotten there so quickly that I knew the customer might still be standing at the phone booth gathering his things together and sighing with resignation, believing that his cab might never show up. Customers do that frequently, especially when the weather is bad, or when cabs are tied up because there's an NBA championship game being played by the Denver Nuggets. That never happens frequently, believe me.

I glanced at my wristwatch and noted that barely a minute and a half had passed since I had taken the call. This was what ultimately kept me inside my taxi. Nobody in their right mind would expect a cab to show up that fast. The fare might even be at the snack counter buying cigarettes or a cup of coffee before going to the door and peering out to see if his cab had arrived.

That was what I was thinking.

I was fabricating scenarios. I was making excuses for my fare who had yet to appear in the doorway, which was really starting to annoy me. I dislike being annoyed at fares because they give me money, and I like people who give me money. It's the instant gratification in me. It makes me impatient with people who don't give my inner brat what it wants right now!

Then a thought occurred to me that made my heart sink. What if another cabbie—say a Yellow Cab driver—just happened to be at Union Station when my call came over the radio and he had stolen my fare? I know how that works. I've done it plenty of times at the mall. I hate it when other people treat me the same way I treat them—it makes me feel like such a commoner.

I began to audibly curse the Yellow Cab company when suddenly my back door opened and a man climbed in wearing a snap-brim hat and a trench coat. He scared the hell out of me.

I reached to the breast pocket of my T-shirt where I keep a nasal-spray bottle filled with ammonia, but let's not delve too deeply into that.

"Did you call a cab?" I said.

"Yes," he said in a voice so husky that I thought he had a cold.

"Is your name ...?" I started to say, but I abruptly stopped. "What's your name?" I said feeling clever.

"Zelner."

"Where to, Mr. Zelner?" I said, dropping my flag and turning on the meter.

He reached inside his trench coat and began digging around for something. Not a gat I hoped. Maybe a nasal-spray bottle. I reminded myself not to loan him my own bottle. I had learned that the hard way.

He pulled out a small square of paper and held his arm across the front seat. "I need to go here," he said. I glanced at his face as he spoke. He had a ruddy face. He looked older than me, for what that's worth. I'm forty-five. His hat was dripping water. It occurred to me that he might have been standing in the rain all this time waiting for me. This made me wonder why he hadn't come dashing to my taxi as soon as I pulled up at the stand.

I switched on the overhead light to read the paper. This threw his face into shadow. The address was right across the Valley Highway in North Denver, at place called Diamond Hill, a small business park.

"Is this very far?" he said.

"No, sir," I said, putting the cab into gear. "Maybe five minutes away."

He sighed with what I took to be satisfaction, pocketed the paper, and sat back. I turned on my headlights and pulled out of Union Station. Already I was thinking what a sweet deal this was. I would probably earn five dollars from this ride, and after I dropped him off I could swing down to the Valley Highway and head north to Interstate 70 and over to the cab company—or the "motor" as we drivers call it—and sign out with at least ten minutes to spare. This was the kind of ideal situation that cabbies are always hoping for. It rarely happens, but when it does happen you have to milk it for all the joy you can get. When you drive a taxi for a living, you rarely get the opportunity to feel ecstatic.

"Is it permissible to smoke inside your taxicab?" Mr. Zelner said, as we pulled away.

I glanced in the rearview mirror and nodded a preamble to saying yes. I was using the power of positive body language to indicate to him that I was amenable to anything that would increase the size of my tip. "Yes sir," I said. "There's an ashtray in the armrest on the door."

"Thank you," he said. He spoke very slowly and distinctly with a foreign accent. By foreign I mean European, although I do realize that Europe itself is not a country in spite of attempts by tyrants throughout history to alter that construct.

I heard the rustling of fabric, the faint scrape of fingers dealing with cellophane, then the man leaned forward and said, "I am sorry but I do not seem to have any matches. Is it possible that you have matches or a lighter that I might make use of?"

"Yes, sir," I said. I reached for my toolbox and popped the lid open. I keep all sorts of things in my box, like matches, small change, toothpicks, pocket Kleenex, anything that might feasibly increase the size of my tips.

I had to refrain from saying, "Want me to smoke it for you, pal?" That's an army joke guaranteed not to increase the size of your tips. I've often wondered whether "army joke" is an oxymoron, but let's move on.

I handed him a book of matches and told him to keep it. I pick up free matches at 7-11 stores, even though I don't smoke cigarettes, although I used to. I pass the matchbooks along to people who are trying to give up smoking. Name anybody who smokes—I guarantee you that he's trying to give it up. The only reason I succeeded at giving up the habit is because I have always been good at giving up.

"Interesting odor," I said, complimenting his smoke. "What brand is that?"

"Gauloise," he replied hoarsely.

I nodded as if I knew what a golwoss was, then headed down to Speer Boulevard and took the 14th Street viaduct across the valley. We were halfway across when I saw a flash of red lights in my rain-spattered rear window. They had come on suddenly, as opposed to appearing in the far distance the way emergency vehicles often do, such as fire trucks and ambulances. I groaned inwardly, then glanced at my speedometer. I was doing the speed limit. Obeying the law is a habit I got into the same day I received my taxi license fourteen years ago. It's one of my better habits. Given the fact that most habits are performed unconsciously I figured that obeying the law would be a good habit to nurture assiduously. But I still groan when red lights flash on. Habit.

"What is that?" Mr. Zelner said, turning around and peering out the rear window.

"I believe it's a police car, sir," I said, as I took my foot off the accelerator.

"Why is a police car following us?" he said in a voice that communicated suppressed panic. I am familiar with that voice. I practically invented it. If you ever want to hear it, just call my answering machine.

"I don't know," I said. "I must have violated a traffic law."

I had no intention of pulling over and stopping in the middle of a viaduct under wet weather conditions, so I gave my brakes a couple of taps and turned on my right blinker to signal to the policeman that I was aware of his presence. I intended to pull into a gas station at the west end of the viaduct.

"Can you elude him?" Mr. Zelner said.

"What?" I said.

"I am late for an appointment."

I glanced at the rearview mirror. Mr. Zelner was turned almost completely around, peering at the red lights of the cop car that was perhaps thirty feet behind my taxi.

"I have to stop, sir," I said. "I can't try to elude a policeman. I would lose my license."

He turned around and looked at me. Then he began touching the pockets of his coat. For one second I thought he was going for a gat. By now we were at the far end of the viaduct and I had to take care of the business of pulling into the station and parking beneath a roof that protected the gas pumps and possibly diving out of my taxi. I could hear Mr. Zelner making rustling noises in the backseat. As I wheeled into the parking lot I glanced at the mirror and saw him tamping out his cigarette. He closed the ashtray and twisted around to look at the cop car that had parked directly behind me.

"This is a local policeman, yes?" Mr. Zelner said, turning and facing front.

I craned my head around and looked into the backseat. His arms were folded and one hand was touching his chin. I forget which hand. The only thing I remember is what his body language communicated: he was prepared to bolt. I had seen this before in other passengers, which we cabbies refer to as "runners." These are people who hop out of a backseat at intersections and run away without paying. I don't know who the genius was who invented the word "runner," beyond the fact that he must have been a taxi driver. I suppose that many a hired coachman in Auld Angland must have chased "runners" down the foggy streets of London town.

"Yes," I said. "It's a Denver Police Department car."

He nodded, closed his eyes, and bowed his head as if to hide his face. His body language was freaking me out, especially the syntax of his skull.

I faced forward, rolled down my window, and prepared myself mentally for the excruciating experience of signing a traffic ticket. You know what I'm talking about. Don't even try to kid me.

"Good evening, officer," I said.

"Good evening, sir," he said. "The reason I pulled you over is to let you know that your left-rear taillight is out."

I started to say, "It is?" but I had been trying for years to wean myself from the habit of making cops repeat themselves. "I wasn't aware of that," I said.

He nodded. "I'm not going to give you a ticket. I just wanted to let you know about it." He ducked his head and glanced into the backseat. "Running a fare?"

"Yes, officer."

"All right. You might be able to buy a replacement bulb in this station. If not, you better get that taken care of as soon as possible."

"I'll do that. Thank you, officer."

He tapped the bill of his cap and said goodnight, then walked back to his car.

As he pulled away and drove up Speer Boulevard, I started thinking about the break he had given me. If I had been a civilian he probably would have ticketed me, but cops always seem willing to give cab drivers a break. Cops and cabbies have a lot in common. We drive automobiles on the job, we work the mean streets, and we frequently deal with weird strangers. The list is almost endless but it's not. At the bottom of the list is the fact that cab drivers don't carry .38 caliber revolvers. At least I don't. Bottled ammonia is as far as the Founding Fathers were willing to let me go.

"I'll take you up to Diamond Hill first, sir," I said glancing at the mirror. "Then I'll come back here and replace the light bulb."

He didn't say anything. I put the transmission into gear, pulled out onto the street, and made my way up to the business park in silence. I thought about turning on my Rocky Cab radio and listening to the dispatcher, but I decided against it. My fare would be getting out in a couple of minutes, and after I replaced the bulb I would be heading back to the cab company to sign out for the night, so I wasn't interested in listening to the perpetual drone of addresses on the receiver. I would opt for AM radio as soon as I was alone, which is what I usually am when I rock to the Stones.

Another option would have been to fill the silence by starting a conversation with Mr. Zelner so that we could drift idly down The Pointless River to The Sea of Forgotten Chatter. But I hate talking to people as it is, and I saw no reason to jump-start a conversation with a man who would be getting out of my backseat in less than two minutes. When you've driven a taxi as long as I have, you get good at estimating how long it will take before a fare climbs out of a backseat. I'm usually right to within a range of ten to fifteen seconds. I'm not bragging, just stating a scientific fact.

But I was wrong.

Mister Zelner would not be climbing out of my backseat within two minutes. He would never be climbing out of my backseat. I guided my cab into an asphalt parking lot and stopped in front of a building. I looked at the meter, switched on the overhead light, and turned around in the seat.

"Three-twenty," I said, meaning three dollars and twenty cents. Mr. Zelner appeared to have fallen asleep. I won't insult your intelligence by pretending that I did not know he was dead. I knew it as soon as I looked at him. I will admit it was odd that I knew he was dead, because the only other dead body I knew of that I had encountered "on the job" was in a mortuary. I was delivering flowers for a living at the time. But since it was a mortuary I had no problem figuring out that the horizontal body on the clinical table was a corpse. However on that rainy night in April I felt psychic as I looked at the fare in my backseat. I felt every hair on my body stand erect. I don't want to get grotesque here but I mean every hair, and I sport a ponytail.

There was something about the way he was sitting that told me he was a goner. He wasn't just slouched against the backseat with his chin resting on his chest with a bit of drool hanging from his lower lip, while his partly curled palms lay slack on his lap. He looked "crumpled." I guess that's where the phrase "crumpled corpse" comes from.

I got out of the driver's seat fast.

I leaned down and looked through the window and said loudly, "Mister Zelner, we're here!" But I did not say it loud enough to wake the dead.

CPSIA information can be obtained
at www.ICGtesting.com
Printed in the USA
FSOW02n0927180615
8080FS